He/She

Books by Herbert Gold

NOVELS

Birth of a Hero
The Prospect Before Us
The Man Who Was Not With It
The Optimist
Therefore Be Bold
Salt
Fathers
The Great American Jackpot
Swiftie the Magician
Waiting for Cordelia
Slave Trade
He/She

STORIES AND ESSAYS

Love and Like
The Age of Happy Problems
The Magic Will

MEMOIR

My Last Two Thousand Years

He/She

A novel

by Herbert Gold

ARBOR HOUSE
NEW YORK

For Don Fine,
good counselor and friend

Part / I

1 .

THE TWO of them celebrated Saturday morning as best they could. She had come back from sitting in the sun in the children's garden of the Congregational Church at the corner, where the young mothers watched their babies crawl and play and they talked about this evident progress in the lives of babies and about their husbands and about taking up their careers, or at least getting jobs soon, after some early birthday for the child, so that life could give them more than it now gave an impatient young mother. He had come back from a Saturday morning meeting at the Board of Education. The racial balance of his school was changing in the usual direction and what could the System do about it?

She said she knew they weren't going to find a solution to racial balance this morning, but did they?

He agreed they had not found an answer and perhaps Saturday should not have to start with a meeting downtown. "But now I'm home," he said, "are you glad to see me?"

"Sort of," she said. At this moment in her life it seemed very important to her to name the exact truth about what she felt and wanted, what she didn't feel and didn't want.

He looked gloomy. He used to look concerned, but now he merely looked gloomy. Naming the exact truth was difficult because she was only slowly coming to knowledge of it herself. And in the meantime, while she was figuring things out—life is impossible, yet here we are—she hated to deal with his earnest, near-sighted looks of concern, gloom, and confusion. And besides, she herself preferred that life be filled with love and kindness and enthusiasm and something which she once named 'unboredom.' So why shouldn't she do her best to make their marriage what he claimed it was, in his moments of enthusiasm —a festival?

Even this truth-telling young wife and mother was tempted to see if festival is still possible. She pulled his thumb boldly in an old private courting joke that had to do with a nursery rhyme, thumbs, plums, and what a good boy was he. "Oh, come on," she said, "the baby's taking a nap."

So the two of them celebrated Saturday noon as best they could. He was always grateful for festival. For her it had once seemed almost as simple, but it no longer was; and until she spoke, finally uttered the No in her heart, she was merely burying its whisper temporarily in the noise of her body which he seemed so proud to summon. He was so brave in his momentary achievement. How could she tell him that a trivial thing does not alter an essential thing?

The sounds of her pleasure, no, his pleasure, their sounds together poured into them, made them one quaking body of earth, slimy with body juices, with happiness that dried on them. It prickled like invisible feathers as it dried, feathery tufts. He

4

liked its smell on them, but she jumped into the bath afterward and he joined her. He put oil on her shoulders and breasts, spreading it with the palms. "Mustn't dry out," he said, "that tender young skin and flesh."

"Mustn't," she said, both of them then wet and oily on the crumpled sheets. "And mustn't start again just now, either, Mister."

But as she said this, she put her legs close to his, and then opened, opened them slowly, skin and flesh. Let the animal awaken. He might have rested. "Oh, I'd do anything for you," he said—it just came out that way as he flung himself over her.

"Sounds like you're talking about the wonderful mother that raised you," she remarked, but then relented: "I'd do *something* for you. This, for instance. Is it enough?"

He sighed and shook.

She sang: He'd do anything for her and she'd do anything for him, so strange was their momentary devotion. . . .

"What?" he asked.

"You inspire song in me," she said.

And he would astonish the world with his power when his wife gave him such words and deeds. In addition, he would do such things as would raise him in the esteem of the Board of Education. He didn't need a melody for her tune.

"Oh, ouch, oh," she said.

She liked hugs sometimes. It was an animal comfort, the warmth of a hug. What she didn't like was the kisses that sometimes spilled in among the hugs. That pressing, that spit, ugh. He felt her dismay. That tonguing and teething and that, oh, closeness; no, she preferred not that, and she could certainly do without the hug if the kiss had to come with it.

He, on the other hand, remembered how his kisses used to make her blush with pleasure, and the little freckling which appeared like sunburn when she was aroused, the perking and freckling and capillary explosion of her body when they made love and it pleased her. So he still wanted to kiss her along with the hugs. He wanted to continue what, it seemed to him, had once been properly started. He liked making love to her on Saturday mornings, when he wore washed and faded blue jeans and a washed and faded blue shirt and no shoes or socks, and she wore washed and thinned-by-washing white jeans, and one of his old white shirts, and no shoes or socks, and they undressed each other slowly, carefully, not laughing at this serious work until it was done, and then they began to laugh, sloshing about in the tub, soaping each other, losing the soap, finding it, laughing; and she raised one leg and put it imperiously on the edge of the tub; he kneeled to dry it and kiss it and it became sleek with kissing . . .

Well, those Saturday mornings are over now, aren't they? Anyway, with a child running about, toddling up for attention, not liking locked doors, those Saturday mornings would be finished anyway, wouldn't they?

They certainly were now.

She had a long reddish freckled body with a bony nose and round blue eyes and large, strong teeth. It didn't sound beautiful; it was. She walked with a slight roll, as if she had no doubts. She smiled, laughed, listened, and fell asleep in an instant, as if she had no doubts. But the strange thing was that she had doubts. She cried twice a month. She said she was lonely. When he asked for what, she used to say, when she loved him, "Nothing," and she clung to him. He comforted her. Deeply he comforted himself in comforting her. When he asked her why those tears, when it seemed that she loved him no longer, she also answered, "Nothing, no reason, nothing." But this year she did not cling to him. And he could not comfort her. And he could not comfort himself.

"What can I do?" he asked her as the slow rain of tears

steadily rolled down her face.

"Why don't you just say it's my period?"

He tried to put his arms around her. Her elbows multiplied. He said, "You used to cry sort of gustily, speedy-like."

"I don't remember," she said.

"Do you remember it used to help if I held you?"

"Go ahead," she said. "You can try." And his arms around her held the tall reddish healthy person who was not intended for slow dripping tears. But the tears continued. Between them there was a cold draft of unlit logs in a dead fireplace.

"There's something I've got to talk with you about," she said.

"Go ahead," he said.

"Oh, my dear, is this the time? Can I do it? When I just can't stop crying like this?"

He held her and waited. Love was too good for me, he thought. It was good enough for animals and people in stories, if not in life, but it was more than he deserved. "Do you love me?" he asked her.

She smiled and shrugged and her eyes were wet.

"Tell me."

She smiled again.

"Does that mean you do?"

She didn't answer, but she touched his arm, his shoulder, she draped those long arms around him. Heat radiated from both their bodies and fumed between them like the sweep of air between lit logs in a fireplace. He took that for an answer. But probably he shouldn't have. It meant, he thought, she wanted to love him. It also meant, he thought, she was trapped and didn't know how to get out.

2

"HELLO *here*. Hello *there*. Hello *every*where."

What sweetness to make a child laugh.

He lay on the carpet, later that Saturday evening, playing sleepily with their sleepy daughter, aware of the long cool white pillars of his wife's legs as they moved about the room, first here, then there, and the mandibles above whisked away papers, child's things, dishes. That sweet, milky, humid smell and taste of a child's neck. It was past her bedtime. His wife never compromised on neatness in the house, despite the birth of their daughter, and had developed these busy whisking gestures against the flood of loose things, wet things, dirty things.

He loved the small person gurgling on his chest. He loved the cool white pillars of legs and the tall person upon them, although he had wished for a year now that she would stop whisking so briskly. He felt sleepy, the warm baby nestling against his shoulder, and some important intelligence deep inside told him it was an exceptionally bad idea for him to be sleepy just now.

"Put her away. It's her bedtime," his wife said. "And then I want to talk to you."

"*With* you," he said, trying for good-humored pedantic grumpiness, but his heart was leaden. He cut short the long cuddle and tickle which was the ceremony of bedtime for Cynthia. His job was to put her down and tuck her in. The child was nearly asleep, anyway, and lay contented, shined her immense blue mirrors on him, shut them and was gone.

He returned and sat opposite his wife, who was for once at rest, her hands folded in her lap. But when he sat down, she stood up. "I used to think we should arrange so I can go out and get a job," she said.

"Agreed. No problem."

"You interrupted. That's not the deal anymore. There are things I want and I don't want. I'd like to be good to you, for example, and I want to punish you. I'd like to be good to me. That's a big one I haven't figured out yet. I'd like it if life really were a festival, dear. But all I know is I have to climb off and out and free of saying good-by to you in the morning, taking care of the kid, plotting a future I can barely glimpse, saying hi, you again, when you come home, and day after day—day after day!"

"We'll change things," he said.

"Quiet! Listen for a change! It's not too complicated. It all comes down to something simple. I don't know what works, but what I do know is this doesn't, this *doesn't* anymore, and now I think it never did. I'm sorry, truly truly truly sorry . . . . You see how simple it is?"

"No," he said. "You've cut the speech down till it's too short."

"I've been practicing," she said. "I don't need this anymore. I need out. I'm not sure what I want, but I need something else.

I have some ideas. It's time for me to move on."

"*What?*" he asked, and joined her in standing.

"I'm sure you're very nice," she said, "and perhaps you'll take this personally. I don't mean it that way. I just mean I don't want you. I think that's enough for a while."

He said What again, he sat down again, he stood up again.

"You can stay in the house," she said, "if you prefer, as long as you understand this."

He stopped and looked at her while his blood, his lymph, his bile, his dinner rushed in different and opposing directions. There was a pounding in his forehead and he had to find a way to let it out. She was waiting. Finally he said, "But I love you."

She sighed. She was afraid of something like this. She had thought it through for months, whisking all the elements about in her head, until she was sure this belonged there and that belonged here, but she had always known he would refuse to deal with how neat and organized she was. It's hard enough to be clear when the subject is so unclear, and worse when she had to explain to a man who doesn't want to understand, who is very stubborn, whose intentions had grown so different from hers. He was working comfortably into a career and a family. The marriage had worked her uncomfortably into nothing, into worse than nothing, into distraction, responsibility, and bondage. And now, with all these burdens, and the burdens were so much more endless than the words about them, she also had to deal with telling him the obvious and the unnecessary. He was obliging her to put it in simple language suitable for a husband.

"I don't love you," she said.

"You loved me," he said.

She shook her head. "Perhaps I did. You remember these things better than I do. You remember *your* things, anyway. All I know is I'm going to be honest with you now."

"You mean this is all?" he asked.

She shrugged.

"No explanation? No effort? No . . ." His voice trailed off. No hope? no chance? no regret?

"No reproach," she said. "I don't want to blame you. You're the way you are and I'm the way I am."

"You haven't said—"

"I spoke all I wanted to speak. You couldn't change. I didn't see how you could change, anyway. And anyway, as you so often tell me, it's a matter of feeling, isn't it?"

He was silent. There was a smell of anxiety, his own; fear, his own; sweat, his own; and when they both were silent like this, it was as if he were far away, watching, listening, smelling the terror he emitted like the smell of sour milk. He said to her: "What about Cynthia?"

"Oh, shit," she said. "You're following all the patterns."

He advanced on her with blackness in his head, and heard her voice explaining, "Hitting me would be part of the pattern, too. I wouldn't forgive that."

He stopped. "Let me just put my arms around you," he said.

She nodded. He did so. He heard his heart thumping against his chest, against her. To his surprise, he felt her heart equally thumping hard. She hugged him. He tried to pull her onto the couch. She tapped his back in a wrestler's release signal. "Please, please," she said softly.

He let her go and they sat together on the couch. After a while he said, "We have to talk."

She sighed. "I've been working it out for a year, more, ever since Cynthia was born."

"You should have mentioned it to me. We should have talked."

"You would just confuse me." She smiled brilliantly with her large, even teeth. "You're so smart. You're so convincing." She patted his arm in friendly fashion. "And I also thought you might try to persuade me."

He gazed at her in amazement and admiration. How well she neatened everything up in her own mind. She paid only the attention of annoyance to how things were not so neat in the rest of life, outside her mind.

"I thought you might hit me," she said. "Thank you for being so reasonable. Thanks for listening."

He was not yet alive. He was still asleep. So she didn't know him through and through. "Just tell me," he said thickly.

"Because you're being reasonable," she said, "I'll try. But it makes me upset when I think about it. If I get angry, it's not you anymore, it's what I think about you and us."

"Don't worry," he said. "Don't explain. Just tell me."

"Okay." She stood up. She seemed to want to talk to him from above, from a distance. Well, that was natural. That was what she wanted. She paced back and forth on her long strong elegant legs. "I'm thirty," she said, "thirty-one in six weeks, and I only feel like half a woman. I spent my twenties with you and I want to be free now."

"That's a conclusion," he said, "not an explanation."

"You like words too much, darling."

"You use them in different ways, darling. Can we avoid sarcasm?"

"Can you avoid reproach?"

"No."

"Then no, dear." She waited. Okay, he didn't interrupt. She would go on. "I only feel like half a woman," she repeated, and he knew this was the way she had been formulating matters to herself, whisking the ideas back and forth until everything seemed neat, provided no one disturbed things again: "I suppose I have fantasies of fulfillment in freedom, that's how you would put it, sarcastically. Oh, I like you, really like you very much in a kind of way—that's sort of vague—and this last year has been hard for you, I know—"

"I thought it was because of the baby—"

"Well, there were times when I really felt, oh, friendly, and I had to restrain myself from being how you wanted me to be because, because, because—"

"Because?"

"Because if I was loving, you would think I loved you. And inside I was trying to separate myself. But I wanted to be loving sometimes, but I didn't dare, I didn't want to mislead you. I suppose you can't sympathize with that."

"I can't even understand it. That's from outer space."

"You're intelligent. You try to think ahead sometimes, too. I knew, try to get this straight, I knew I'd be sorry tomorrow if I gave way to these sort of tender feelings I had for you today. Like going to a movie and having dinner and a walk and holding hands—oh, have a little feeling for me, too, can you? Sometimes I wanted to do those things with you, but that would have been cruel. You'd have expected it again tomorrow."

H "I was a junkie for love."

S "I couldn't understand how you put up with me. You were trying to get blood from a stone. Well, it wasn't always stone. It was petrified. This is ancient history, dear. I hoped you would make this hard decision I have to make now—do everything around here, don't I? You would choose to find some tasty thing, someone more agreeable, maybe even prettier, there are lots— you would just walk out on me."

H "I love you."

S "Oh, shit. I was afraid of that."

H "I was waiting because I thought with a child, turning thirty, all the changes—"

S "That was kind of boring of you, darling. I didn't marry you for your patience."

"I loved you."

"I guess you did."

He tried to be sensible with the craziness, it wasn't even pain yet, in his head. "Why don't we talk to someone?" he asked. "How about therapy? I think we need it."

"I already did. I talked with Sandra Block. She does Gestalt. I told her I was confused, I don't love you anymore and I don't know what to do, I feel it was all a mistake, and she said I'm not confused then, I know what I want, and I should fulfill my needs if that's how I perceive them."

"That's how you perceive them."

"Not necessary to be sarcastic, my dear. It's a summary. The words might be silly, but if you think I'm silly, that should make it so much easier for you. A sweet tasty agreeable thing with more agreeable words. The point is: what I need is freedom at this stage."

Different stages from hers existed simultaneously in his head. He had been disappointed, patient, yes, even sometimes bored with her since their daughter was born, but he had thought this merely an interlude of diapers and fatigue and sly entrapment by parenthood. Beneath these temporary pulsations, there was a stronger rhythm of blood—they loved each other. Their earlier times together were as real as the anxious patience of the past year. How ardently she had helped him to court her. Her sleek and amused inventiveness in bed (on floor, in motel, in sleeping bag, behind curtains, in a museum closet). Her determination to get married. Her efficient informing and arranging with parents, grandparents, friends (she whisked about then, too, explaining very precisely to family and printers exactly what she had in mind).

How could one not fall silent, as he did now, in admiration of her efficiency? As efficiently as she performed falling in love, reaching climax, getting pregnant, so would she be equally efficient in arranging an amicable, friendly, sensible divorce.

It was, however, not his way to remain silent with admiration.

"Don't you remember?" he asked weepily. This was the beginning of the prayer he would deliver many times during the next month. Don't you remember the ferry rides, the sleepy weekends in a fogbound seaport, the private jokes, the popcorn-groping privacy of movies, the pride in getting ready to have a child, the pride in having the child, the—

"That was then," she said. "This is now. I'm different."

He looked at her, tears on his face, sincere tears, absolutely intent tears, but he also hoped the baby would not awaken and interrupt this interrogation. Babies interrupt frequently, without consideration of work responsibilities or adult emotions. The child took no notice when he brought home a heavy briefcase. He wondered about the chance of the baby awakening—time to clean baby, time to diaper baby—and then he would have to restart sincere lachrymose glands and continue discussion of disaster, pain, suffering, dread, longing, and a woman's requirements as she crosses into her thirties.

She was giving him advice. "I respect your feelings," she said. "I don't respect blubbering."

That stopped him.

"I cried myself sometimes. Once I burst into tears when I was talking to Sandra in her office and she said, Just get it out, just let it all come." She looked at him speculatively. "So I suppose if you want to blubber, then blubber away."

"How did I stop you from being free? What did I do that meant you couldn't be yourself? When were you seeing this Sandra Block?"

"A couple of Thursday afternoons," she said. "How would you know? Maybe it was just me in this situation. I looked around, I saw attractive hunks of guys, they looked at me, but what they saw was an uptight young matron, they didn't know what was going on underneath. I couldn't let them have an opening. I didn't know how."

He wondered if she could have had an affair and worked it through and thus saved their marriage, might still, so he said: "Why didn't you just have an affair, work it through, and then we'll see?"

This touched her. She knew he wasn't so blithe. He really meant to do anything he could for her. She was moved. She said: "Too late for that. Not my style, anyway. Now don't start crying again, you'll wake Her."

They often spoke of the child with this capitalized pronoun She or Her.

"Aren't you yourself?" he asked. "Weren't you always?"

"I felt like half a woman. I said that already."

"You did."

"It's the truth. I guess it just leaks out. I don't mean to bore you. Oh, dear," she said, "you can't stop crying, can you?" and reached for him, and they kissed, and they pulled and tugged at each other, and they scratched and bit and sucked, and they ran with sweat, and they rolled on the floor, and he didn't know what else to do for her, tears do no good, and she didn't know what else to do for him, good sense does no good, and they didn't know what else to do for each other, and when it was over and they lay peacefully in each other's arms, the war suspended, the struggle over, the ache assuaged, the tears stopped with desire and pleasure, then she said: "Maybe I just can't sustain a relationship."

3

BEFORE SHE made her decision, there had been a lovely radioactive glow emitted by her efficient tall factory of a body. She did everything. She did the house and the child and the checkbook and the closets. For months she even did her pleasure with him with stealthy speedy whirring efficiency. And then she slept. Her heart was sheathed from harm by him, from contact with him. It seemed that her eyes and ears and body were protected, but in fact they were exposed; it was her heart that was burrowing away through earthworks and preparing for demolition.

It came.

Good-by comes before farewell and yet nothing comes after good-by. First she made her decision and then she acted on it. Nothing to do with him. It came all by herself, a solitary come.

Because she was a reasonable and generous person, she allowed him to inflict the boredom of explanation on her. He demanded it. She would have to live through all this, too. She sighed and said, "I guess I don't love you anymore. No, that's not right. I *don't* love you anymore. No." She thought again. She wanted to get the matter precisely right. "When I look back on it, I never loved you."

"Not possible. Can't you remember? Ask anyone."

"I'm not talking about what people thought they saw or even what I pretended. I'm not talking about what you wanted, what you thought you felt. I'm talking about what I remember. I'm sorry."

"Sorry?"

"I imagine this is hard on you."

"I can't even understand what you're saying. I don't recognize you."

"Try," she said. "You better," she said.

He tried to be cunning. He was fighting for his life, wasn't he? He tried to pick an irresistible subject and an invincible manner. "Kids frown on parents breaking up," he said. He wanted to kill.

"Parents are people. God meant them to survive."

"I'm preventing your survival?"

"Yes."

He wanted to die. He said: "You talk like a fucking growth machine," and before she could ask what the devil that meant, he added: "I don't know what I'm saying. Who are you? Who are you? Who *are* you, wife?"

"That's just the point," she said calmly. "I need to find out. As you notice, with you I'm unrecognizable as a person. That's the very point, dear."

"It's bad," he said.

"I know I've been a no-good wife who deserves to be left and dumped. So why don't you leave me and dump me? I agree to that. I'll agree to as much of this talk as you need, provided it's not more than I can stand. I'll go on for a while but it does no good. It wrecks."

"Why?" he asked. "What?"

"I can't divorce myself," she said. "I can't even divorce our child. I've got to divorce someone."

He watched her hands fluttering against her thighs.

"I hate all this talking. I knew it would be like this. It stopped me for months that I knew you'd insist I explain and explain and I hate it. This shall we say and let's assume. This now wait and listen and make it clear. Oh shit. It's not that I don't really like you, but I'll start hating you if I have to explain and explain and explain."

"Just tell me."

"I did."

"Look at me and see if you can tell me."

He fixed her eyes with his. He burned his hope of survival and his desperation into her. He wondered if anyone could resist so much need. She said softly: "I want out, dear. Get that through your fucking dumb please dear head. And furthermore," she said, with a long unwilling breath, because it seemed necessary for her at that moment to say it: "I think I have a lover."

"You *think?*"

"I'm trying to tell the truth. I have a lover, I think."

"Who?"

"No, no, no."

He pretended it was a game of twenty questions. This meant he didn't have to think yet about her having a lover, but only about who it was. He tried to guess.

"What difference does it make?" she asked.

He shouted names. He spattered out the roll of their friends, wanting to kill each one, all of them. She looked frightened.

"No, no, no. That's not the point," she said.

"Are you crazy?" He realized there was spittle on his mouth.

"Are you? Why don't you pay attention to what I'm saying?"

"Why can't I know?"

"Please, please, please," she said. "It's not part of it at all. That's not what I'm trying to tell you. It's not what you need to know. It doesn't even matter!" she screamed.

A cunning thought came to him. If he couldn't know, and didn't know, and she didn't even want him to know, or she only wanted him to know, then it was all still between him and her and the lover made no difference. It was, he was, they were just part of her new enterprise, but her husband was still her man.

"I can't stand this," she said, and very sensibly needed a bath. He very foolishly stood sweating and waiting outside the locked door. He tried to make love to her when she got out of the shower. She hit him with a hair brush and he put up his arm to protect himself and the hair brush broke. This was an attempted rape followed by an attempted assault. Then he wept and she said, "I know I'm being selfish, but that's how it is. You're so strong I can't get what I want without being selfish."

"Okay," he said, not believing all this. It sounded like flattery which he didn't deserve or need.

"I want you to stay with Cynthia this weekend. I'm going away."

"Where? why?"

She was making disgusted clicking noises with her mouth. "I want to go away with someone," she said.

Ice in his breast. "Okay," he said. "I'll stay with her. We'll have fun together."

"Atta boy," she said. "I'm sorry, I'm really sorry, this must be hard on you, but this is how it is."

"I keep repeating myself," he said.

"So do I," she said.

That's calm, that's nice, he thought. Good lad.

So she packed a little overnight bag and smiled a sickly smile and he held up their child to be kissed and he waved to her from the window and what the hell were they doing? This was a continuation of the patience which had bored her, which had surely made her most impatient. He was paralyzed by wanting her and not having her and waiting. She drove rapidly, expertly, up the street, and disappeared around the corner and the baby began to cry.

Thank God. He busied himself with taking care of Cynthia.

Toys.

Food.

Cleaning.

So this is a househusband, he thought.

And my wife has gone off to spend a weekend with her lover. Of course he will smell new and fresh, and the grain of his beard is different under her fingertips, and his bed will be strange and exciting, and his weight other than mine, and when she instructs him about what she likes, it will be a voyage of discovery for both of them. He began to imagine their play in some cozy bachelor pad—who? what? where? when?—but thank God this imagined news story was interrupted by Cynthia and his heart overflowed with gooey love for their child and he nuzzled her with his unshaven chin and she gurgled and giggled and he wept. He put his head between his knees and choked on hopeless helpless sobs. And this was interrupted by changing her diaper. In the bathroom mirror he caught sight of himself, barefoot, frazzled, nearly ten pounds down from his weight of a few weeks ago, carrying between two fingers a shitty diaper. And thus his sobs had not been hopeless and helpless after all, because he was doing what had to be done about the diaper of a child who was reaching the age when she would soon stop using a diaper. And that's one of the worst times for diapers.

It's realler than a flag, he thought.

The foot-faced President was going on television to Explain.

He looked at the sincerely evading eyes, the marionette elocutionary gestures, and remembered with astonishment: There is something else in this world besides my fever.

Perhaps he could give himself a cure of generosity and interest in others by turning on the teevee more often. I'm far gone if watching teevee is a sign of improving health.

The day passed. The night passed. He slept on the floor of Cynthia's room. First: he couldn't stand to sleep in their bed without his wife when she was (news story, news story). Second: he wouldn't have to make the bed in the morning. Using a sleeping bag like this was an adventure, a hiking trip, a graduate student during a holiday. No: he was camping out in a death ward.

He dreamt she suffered a crippling automobile accident and he had to nurse her back to health.

He dreamt she was screaming with . . . No, it wasn't pain in this dream, it was pleasure, and he awoke grinding his teeth.

Ah, it's nice to be alone, he thought. Cynthia and me, here together, the two of us, together against the world. Amazing, this weekend when she was museum-going, hiking, swimming, resting in her lover's arms—screaming with joy, as he dreamed it—passed almost without his knowing that the day changed into night, the night into dawn, the dawn into day. Cynthia had never been held so much, hugged so much, and she drooled and crooned at him with gratitude.

It was Sunday night and he heard the garage door opening. A creak, a car engine starting again, stopping again, the garage door closing.

No, he wouldn't run down to welcome her home.

She came poking rather slowly up the stairs. That was odd. Her face was white. That was odd.

She had left her overnight bag downstairs. That was odd.

She smiled at him and shrugged her soulders. "I was sick the whole time," she said. "I couldn't. I just kept on throwing up. It was embarrassing."

He didn't say he was sorry.

"But I wanted to," she said. "Maybe it was just the stomach flu. I sincerely wanted to."

I'm sure you did, he tried to say comfortingly, but it came out: "We had fun, Cynthia and I. She's lovely."

"I suppose you're glad it worked out this way," she said. "I'm not a Modern Woman."

"Yes," he said.

"But I'm trying. Either I or my stomach will give in."

"Yes," he said.

"I'm stronger than my stomach," she said.

"I'm sure you are."

"I will be. Now let's talk and try to get a few things straight." She was laughing. She knew her predicament was ridiculous. She said she couldn't stand it how old-fashioned her stomach was.

For some reason he felt exalted. Whatever had happened, now she really wanted to talk with him. Out of the mouths of failed adulteresses might come the truth. He felt strong in his survival as a single parent, as if he had come out ahead over this Saturday and Sunday and the Friday night before. What do we define as victory in such conflicts? he asked himself.

Straws and portents and a wife's diarrhea.

4

WHAT SHE wanted to talk about was seeing couple therapists. Since he had been urging that they see a doctor, any doctor, a therapist, any therapist, this pleased him. It struck him as a significant admission of his need, his desperation, his hopes and dreams. Evidently her stomach had convinced her that her certainties were not verities. (But what if it was only a virus?) Evidently she still considered their marriage of some importance.

"Who?" he said. "I've asked around already."

"There's a couple, Couple Therapy is what they do, they trained in Gestalt," she said. "I think that's what we could use, a whole new massive way, both of us seeing a couple together, four of us, even if it's kind of expensive."

"Yes, I'm willing," he said mildly, trying to hide his sense of triumph. Not only had she and her stomach neglected to cuckold him, but also it seemed she had positively agreed to rescue their marriage. He would go into debt if necessary. Love is all that matters. Cynthia needed them both.

"I've already called," she said, "and they're willing to see us, as this emergency initial deal, this evening. I've arranged for a sitter."

He was lost in admiration of this woman, his wife. Even if she had a sour upset stomach, at this very moment he wanted to make love, but he was not sure she would understand this expression of his esteem.

"Okay," he said. "I'll drive."

"We'll take my car," she said. "I know the way. It's in the neighborhood where I spent the weekend."

But she didn't tell him exactly where or with whom. Did she want to blindfold his eyes like a kidnap victim? Such things should be clarified in Couple Therapy.

Paul and Paula Glaze, the Gestalt Couple Therapist Team, wanted not to be called Doctor and Doctor, but rather Paul and Paula, because, for one thing, they did not have Ph.D.'s or medical diplomas. Also it was more immediately intimate and upfront for all participants to be on equal terms, sharing their intimate upfront very own first names. Paul took the name "Paul," replacing "Stewart," his wornout old label, in order to symbolize his rebirth when he graduated from his Alcoholics Anonymous program. He had also graduated from the County Drunk Drivers Clinic, where he met Paula, obliged to attend, although she was not a drunk driver, because she had been arrested with her previous Primary Lover driving while under the influence. Her name had been Bernice before she and Paul decided to travel through life and Gestalt as a team, wearing team colors.

He had doubts about Paul and Paula, but anything that kept

them in touch and considering each other might be helpful. The therapists lived in a rumpled old house in a dilapidated section of town. The house was furnished by Goodwill and Salvation Army, foam and protruding springs nakedly honest in the sitting room where clients waited with copies of *Cricket, Parents, Co-Evolution Catalogue,* and a pile of dental hygiene magazines. They heard the couple whose hour preceded theirs screaming and they heard something drop and shatter and they heard Paul shout, "Okay, okay! Violence is probably what you needed to do! But pay for the breakage around here, got it?"

And then the sobs of the annealed couple, and a few minutes later, huddled like grieving refugees, they staggered through the sitting room and out. The woman was crying. The man was comforting her and stroking her bloody hair. The blood came from a cut on his comforting hand.

Paul stood beaming in the doorway. "You must be Him," he said, "and you must be Her. Come meet Paula, she's just washing up a little. We really had a productive session, I suppose you heard. Wow."

Paul was a stocky man with a creased mug and a short-range haze of tobacco shrouding him from close inspection. His belly-button showed through his shirt. He put his cigaret out on the rug beneath his heel after lighting another and beaming at the visitors. Funky Honesty was the message he communicated: Regular Fella. He held absolutely still a moment, saying, "Welcome, welcome!" And then: "Time to commence."

They filed into a sitting room with a variety of sofas, folding chairs, a blackboard, a few books, and a basket of toys. If we wanted to bring in our child, he wondered, would there be a Paulette or a Pauline for triad therapy?

Paul swept aside the shards of glass on the floor with the foot he also used for cigaret extinguishment. "Sit, sit," he said. "I won't start the hour till Paula gets here—*Paula! Paula!* Where the hell are you?"

"Just taking a pee," she said, smilingly buttoning up her fly, an ample woman in sailor pants and a Navy shirt. "One of Paul's problems is he's compulsive about time and money. And he's got to get his nicotine fix, too,"—Paul was lighting up again to signal that the clock was running. There was a smell of cigaret dust—ashtray broken by the previous patients—and new stubs were being put to rest in a coffee cup, sizzling briefly as the butts encountered cold coffee.

Normally he didn't like women who introduced themselves with talk about taking a pee, and finished adjusting their clothes while still talking about it, visiting with the visitors and hitching at the pants, and also he was normally not powerfully attracted by hefties, but Paula had a vigorous, hearty, and friendly look to her. She didn't smoke. Evidently she ate. She sat down and said to Paul: "Okay, I'm ready."

He and She were ready, too.

Paul said, "So tell your lies and we'll try to begin, okay?"

He looked at her and she looked at him and finally he said, "She wants out of our marriage. I want to keep our marriage alive."

"I don't hear words of love," Paul said.

"I just began," he said. "I wanted to give you the basic facts first. I love her."

With a little smile, Paul looked at Paula and said, "Let's stipulate that he says he loves her. How about you?"

"I don't love him anymore," she said, "if I ever did."

Paul twisted in his chair. "And how does that make you feel?"

"Rotten." He felt pressure in his sinus. He didn't want to weep before these strangers. The hour had only begun. "Awful. I don't know why. I was sure she loved me. I'm sure she's wrong in what she says—"

And the tears came. They rushed out.

"Let's stipulate that He cried, Paula. And how does that make You feel?" Paul asked the wife.

"That's his problem," she said. "I don't feel involved when he cries. He's been crying a lot lately. It's his problem."

"That's pretty clear then," Paul said. "That's nice. That's clear. Of course, nothing is really clear—"

Paula's hand shot up. "Wait a sec!" she said. "I'm not satisfied. That's not the whole truth. I think she is hiding deeper feelings, Paul. I think we have to explore this factor."

He felt himself falling in love with hefty Paula. From the beginning he had felt she might be on his side; at least, that he might win her over. He felt he could never win Paul over. She was overweight, but she didn't smoke and she had a crinkly careless earthy face. She had insight. Paula was saying, "I think she is out for hidden goods—"

"—what we call Hidden Goods," Paul explained. "Go on."

"She wants to hurt. She has been hurt herself, of course. In the power flux—"

"What we call Power Flux," Paul explained.

"She feels a shift in her favor. She wants to make the most of it. But I don't think anything is so definite as she wants to say it is. Why is she here? What does she want from us? For her there is hidden goods in the power flux, Paul."

He felt a definite love for Paula, but his wife was turning a face of sweet reason on the therapist. "I'm here because I want to be fair. He begged me to do something. I owe our history together, for some reason we have a history together, to investigate it, even if there's really nothing more to investigate. I tried to have an affair and I threw up the whole weekend."

"Ah," said Paul, "up tight. Why?"

"But now I took some Pepto-Bismol and I feel fine. I called

my lover and he wants to give me another chance. My stomach feels fine."

"And how do you feel about that?" Paul asked the husband. "Do you feel like killing yourself?"

"Something like that. Like dying."

"I gathered as much. Let's stipulate your Hidden Goods is a situation of masochistic revenge and you think you can achieve a Power Flux through suffering. Okay. Now you: If you imagine him killing himself, how does that make you feel?"

"It's not my responsibility," she said. "I didn't do it to him. I'd be sorry, of course."

Sturdy Paula turned gloomy. "How do you feel about killing yourself if you know she doesn't care? Do you still feel like it?"

"I didn't say I was going to kill myself. Paul suggested that. I said I sometimes felt like it. I said I felt more like dying, if I didn't have to do it myself. I realize it would be foolish."

Paul was rubbing his hands. They were getting someplace. "I don't mean to suggest that you kill yourself. That's just a probe. But let's stipulate you're not exactly overcome with the horror of death in this life dilemma," he said. He went on rubbing his hands, making a dry crackling noise, as if his surgeon's washup had dried the skin; and while he rubbed, he stole a glance at his watch to see how much of the hour remained. It was thirty dollars an hour, not a really authoritative fee, but reasonable pay for non-medical helping personnel who had set up in the Gestalt business for themselves.

The husband was wondering what further advice he might get from Paul.

The wife was yawning and covering her mouth. It had been a long weekend.

Outside, a dog was barking for the end of Sunday and a motorcycle was being raced before being tucked into a garage until next Saturday.

"Up," said Paul.

He looked at his wife and then at the ceiling. "Up?" he asked.

"Hour's up," said Paul, getting rid of another butt in the coffee cup.

"I think we should continue a beat or two," said Paula, "since we're finally getting to some basic stuff here and we can stipulate we started late because I took a long pee. Anyway, that watch of yours is fast. We didn't start on the hour."

"Look, Paula, it's not professional to give extra time, goddammit, my watch is fixed now." But then he relented. "Oh, aw right. So where were we? He was killing himself and she cared but not personally—that correct?"

She composed herself for frank avowal. "I used to care about him a lot, but it scared me. I thought I was becoming dependent. That was in the distant past when I got pregnant. I wasn't sure he would be there when I leaned. And in fact, sometimes he wasn't."

"Wasn't?" he asked. "*Wasn't?*" he demanded, his voice rising. "When did I ever? When did I ever fail to show you I? When did I?" he stammered. He was dizzy with confusion, and remorse, and love. "When?"

Paul tapped his watch. "Hey, look," he said. "Now the hour really is up, but answer the question first."

"It's too complicated. I'm not sure I want to get into it," she said.

Paul stood up, putting out one more butt. "Well, we have to explore all this stuff next time. Why is it too complicated and why don't you want to get into it? I think, my dear, it's not so easy as you say. I think you are involved with this man in some way." He winked at the husband. "Though maybe not so much, and in quite the same fashion, as he would prefer. Do you agree, Paula?"

"I reserve," she said. "I think we've opened up some fruitful material, however. She is not as cold as she seems and he—" He began to love Paula a bit less; she definitely had a weight problem. "And he is not such a passionate swain as he imagines himself, now that he is faced with total loss. He has a side of childishness in his desire to keep this marriage going."

"Flux," murmured Paul. "There's our next couple, flushing the toilet already. They always get sick *before* the hour. Everyone has their own way of dealing with it, don't you?"

5

HE OPENED the car door for her. He was broken into silence. "I better not drive," he said thickly, and so she drove, humming. She said at last: "I bet Paul would find this significant."

He rose an inch from his pit and looked at her in the dark. He needed an operation on his brain. He might need his soul removed, but perhaps it wasn't located in his head at all. In his chest. In his belly. Down below.

"My driving, I mean. But then he'd ask us why it's significant and it wouldn't be anymore."

He sank again. She fell silent, but she patted his knee. Good dog. "I'm going to try again," she said.

He started. He didn't believe it. She started to laugh.

"Not what you were thinking. You should know better, with your high intelligence. That was no doubt a virus I had, and the strain of a whole weekend, the strain I've been under. This work

I'm doing, no matter how crude Paul and Paula are, is helping me. I'll try only an afternoon with, with, with . . . "

"This is not helping me."

"You always told me you were smart, darling. You're not acting real smart these days. Why don't you find someone?"

"Because I don't want anyone else." He was aware of a certain slyness in the confession. Because it was abject and true, and yet he had dreamt of a yielding honey-haired girl who lived down the block, whom he had seen, whom he had never spoken to, whom he sometimes dreamed of. "I don't want anybody but you."

She was shaking her head. "Impossible. You're making it difficult. Here I am at this stage in my passage, and you're at another. You're not showing insight and compassion commensurate with your intelligence, my dear."

"I guess you're being sarcastic," he said. "Who is it?"

"Shush. But what about that girl down the block I see you look at? The skinny chick with the thin Clairol hair."

"I don't know any such girl."

"You know her. I may not be as smart as you, but I have some brains, too. But I'm not jealous—"

"I don't want her."

"Want her!"

"I want you."

"I said I'm not jealous. Take what God and the neighborhood suggests. Because this is the way I am."

And she patted his knee again twice. And drove. And he fell into a confused reverie about the woman he had married, an unbroken creature with wild smiles and a gift for throwing herself heedlessly into what she was doing, making a picnic or cleaning a house or climbing up and down his body to discover undiscovered country. Or wrecking an idea with her own ideas. She had been very young. Now she was still young. She still liked to be original. They were home, she had parked, and she was saying very tenderly, "I know this is hard on you. I know I shouldn't be so honest. It's not kind of me. But I've got to do what I've got to do."

It was coming over him again. "Who?"

"Darling," she said. "Darling, don't. Let me tell you something. Feel better, please, darling. I'd make love with you now, only my period's coming and I just really don't feel like it—okay?"

He thought: She'll wait for that afternoon with her lover until her period is over. She likes things to be heedless but neat. So practical like that. So he had a few days' respite.

It's not a damn phantom lover, he thought. Soon I'll know who he is.

The next day at his office—he was assistant principal in an inner-city junior high school, not merely a pained husband—he was attending to business, looking over a report about cost-cutting from the school board's consultants—when his secretary buzzed him to say the visiting Norwegian educator wondered if he could see him a little early. "Invite him to lunch," he said, and the secretary came back to ask: "May he bring his wife?"

He would spend his lunch discussing federal funding with a Norwegian middle-school principal and his wife, who would probably not be interested in the intricacies of protein-balanced kiddie-feeding and racial equilibrium.

He took them to a traditional heavy-wooded hofbrau near the railroad station. It was left over from the time this part of the city was still immigrant European. There were slow-moving mastodon waiters and lamps on the tables with little yellow bulbs in thick brown shades. He remembered the Norwegian, a jolly man of his own age, looking older, bald, with pink lips and the heavy arms and thighs of a neglected athlete. And his wife?

There was an immediate pang. She was long and lean and a coltish girl, but not reddish like his wife—dark and neat, with that Celtic black Irish look, and a long nose and solemn formal smile. She was like a shy graceful formal adolescent dragged along to dinner by daddy. When he squinted at her, he could make out lines around the eyes; she smiled and the lines deepened; but she was wrapped in a childless girlish lost-wife silence. Trouble in Oslo, he thought. "My wife Lauren is an artist," said his colleague Uwe, "however she consented to close up her studio and visit the States with me. It was good of her to give up silk-screening for a few weeks in order to keep me company, yes please, and also good of you—"

"My pleasure," he said, heartfelt.

"Good of you, since I have told her of your charm, my colleague—"

To cut straight to the heart of the matter: this plump, pink, formerly athletic colleague of his, once a skier and a soccer player, was, with European savoir vivre, laying off his wife on him. *Savoir vivre* was not a Norwegian word, but it was the only European language he knew to express his amazement.

"Truth to tell," said the truth-telling Norwegian, "we have resolved our difficulties now. We are being divorced, but we are being still friends. I suppose this seems odd to you."

"Yes. No." He thought again. "Yes."

"You are embarrassed?" the lady asked. "Uwe, you shouldn't say, even if your nice American friend—"

"I'm going through something myself just now," he said.

Uwe beamed. His lips were damp and pink. "So you see. It is a universal matter, like the Napoleonic Code and Roman law, only slightly amended by different customs. The war of the sexes. And the peace treaties. He understands."

Lauren tapped his knee on the place where his consoling wife tapped it when they drove back from Couple Therapy. But the

Norwegian lady struck his knee differently. Lauren's tap was not so comradely. It was not consoling. It was more patient. It was inciting.

"Darling," said Lauren to her husband, "in some places, Africa, South America, even southern Europe, the Napoleonic Code and Roman law are replaced by murder, madness, and cannibalism—different laws, my dear."

And the American added: "There is also Anglo-American jurisprudence."

"Most dangerous of all!" cried the Norwegian. "My friend, are you most dangerous of all? A cannibal to devour human flesh? You like my former wife? My former wife likes you? Am I doing my best to spoil everything?"

"Yes," said Lauren.

"Yes," said the American.

And they finished the bottle of wine, toasting international collaboration in the Hofbrau by the Sea, a family-owned franchise, where murder, madness, cannibalism, and rage were being politely calibrated with the aid of funds and a grant from the Institute for International Education.

6

ENOUGH TWISTING and turning, he thought. Time to do some crying out loud, howling, groaning, barking. I'm still a young dog; or if not so young, a living animal with healthy kibble.

"You would like to see some of this city?" he asked Lauren. Her husband had an appointment with another principal, or perhaps at the school board, or elsewhere, surely elsewhere, where his wife would find it rather dull.

"I would like perhaps to see some of this city?" she echoed him. "Is it not odd how you Americans, so generous, so courteous, seek to put me at ease by mimicking my difficulties with English?"

"I'm sorry. I'll try not to," he said.

"But I was thanking you," she said. "Yes, I would like. To see some reality of the city. You know, when one travels, what one sees is the inside of airplane, then the inside of terminal, hotel, bar, restaurant, museum, theater, some of this very interesting no doubt, touristic, educational—"

"One does," he said.

She gave him a peculiar crooked smile, tipped up at one end, down at the other, an ironic smile on this slender dark Scandinavian woman with the straggle of dry hair over her forehead. "What I would like to see is, as a tourist of course, all I can expect, some authentic American poverty which we hear about. Our neighboring Swedish sociologists study it, Myrdal family you know, we see on the television, but except for the taxi from the airport—"

"I can arrange a reality tour," he said.

"And afterward, because sadness of poverty makes me sad, a nice green park to walk in, to forget pain and ugliness."

"You're a very practical person," he said. "Let me give it some thought. Okay, now I've given it some thought. Near here, your hotel, we can walk to the Tenderloin—"

But they drove. He wanted his car for later. She was telling him he was a unique sort of American, he didn't talk continually about his wife and children, he didn't show her snapshots; and he was saying that was, just now, too long a story, and he was sure she didn't need to hear it; and she said correct, she didn't need, and she didn't want, either, she just hoped to enjoy reality tour—it was fast becoming known as their Reality Tour—and he was smiling and laughing and feeling good. Lauren might be a stranger, but she was nice, smart, and funny. Stranger is unimportant when those other qualities are present and the clock says Now.

The Tenderloin area was a neighborhood of old folks—"senior citizens," he said, "junkies, runaways, welfare 'clients' "—he said "clients"—and hotels with televisions in the lobbies and people watching those televisions without moving or changing the station, even when it snowed and little else on the screen.

42

All-day bars featured nighttime gogo dancing with the bass vibrations from the jukeboxes thudding out to the street. "Come on in, you're eligible, your hands are in your pockets already!" a barker called from a doorway. Neon champagne glasses blinked neon champagne bubbles. Adult bookstores, recycled furniture and clothing shops, fried grease eateries— a used-up American downtown.

"Standard for the U.S.," he said to Lauren.

"Hey, girlie! girlie!" a woman carrying a Raggedy Ann doll shouted at them. She wore a white cardboard shade on her nose to protect it from the sun; her shopping bag said Safeway. "Girlie, you dropped your hook!"

He explained to Lauren what a hooker is. Lauren said, "Very interesting now. Before you translate, her joke means nothing to me."

"It wasn't a joke. It's a crazy."

"Oh, but she is so fill with laughter. Yes, it is mostly not a joke," said Lauren, "and thus your Reality Tour for the ignorant foreign lady has come to its logical end. Now we find a green space, yes?"

He had left his automobile nearby for just this eventuality. They drove to the large urban park—ponds, flower gardens, statues of ethnic heroes, tennis courts, and a dense English garden—and she said, "You do not speak of your wife. Very rare among Americans. I congratulate you."

"Don't congratulate me yet," he said.

"Oh?"

"I think about her."

She patted his arm. "I know. I know you have difficulties. My nose"—she sniffed charmingly—"I have a sensitive nose."

"You don't speak about our friend, your husband, either."

"That is much less unusual," she said. "I am used to not speaking of him, or him of me. We are good friends, however.

43

I imagine you are not such good friends with your wife?"

"No. I love her."

"There, we are doing it, speaking," she said, "and it is all my fault. Enough."

He felt finicky, they emerged from the car, she took a deep breath. "Your cities have these green strips, also these poor people. We have the parks, too, the tram out of Oslo especially." She took his arm and led him forward with one giant step, setting out on a hiking trip. "Now you show me your buffalo." *Boofalo*, she said.

"There are no buffalo here. It's not a zoo."

She laughed. There were teenagers on bicycles sweeping down the curving drive and shouting echo songs at the underpass. "Every park is zoo, my dear friend, with wild animals who are tame in other part of their life-lives. You too seem to have been tame so long, and man is not meant to be such."

"You came to the park to give me a lecture?"

"You brought me to the park because you also have something on your mind, my friend." There was an autumn warmth in the air, sun-warmed air drifting under the trees, and curled against each other like teenagers, in full daylight, under the trees, with a blanket of sun-warmed air circulating above them, they lay on the grass with their arms pressing the back of the opposite stranger. Finally they kissed just once, a long searching kiss. Before his lips brushed her cheek, before he caressed her hair or eyes, before he kissed her hello or good-by or how nice to see you, they were kissing with open mouths searching the wet folds of meat inside. Good, good. And then they just rested. And then their hands and fingers played, searching along thighs, while beyond the bushes, the clipclop of the park police horses clipclopped by.

When they stopped kissing and fell away, gasping like children in the glee of torments they have chosen, he saw a tiny blackened bird body through the bushes; and his eyes, sharpened by excitement, could make out the crawling things carrying away bits of it, so that by next week or next month it would be nothing; and even this did not harm his pleasure—the vision increased it. That's what life is, he thought. That's what death is. So make the most of both of them.

His underwear was twisted. His crotch felt hot. It itched and he worried if an insect had found its way there. He was so happy, happy, he thought; happiness comes with the strangest pangs amid the most grievous forgetfulness. "Lauren," he said. She nodded near his shoulder, as if pleased that he remembered her name. He wanted her to say his name but she did not.

"I guess we better get up," he said.

She didn't move.

"Now?" he said.

She still didn't move. This was better than speaking his name. He believed she did not want their moment of childishness to end.

"We are little people, are we not?" she said.

"It feels good to be with you. You won't believe this—"

"I do, even though it is hard to believe." She ran her fingers through her hair. She brushed his clothes with her hands, and then hers. She sat up. She stood up. She waited for him. She stretched and made a sudden convulsive yawn. "Hard to believe you are playing like this for the first time. But I do believe you are really in love, desperately in love with your wife as I am not with my husband. And that," she said, smiling, "is why I am so much more calm than you, my friend." She took his arm. "We walk, yes? You have strength to visit the recreation park more?"

"You seem to know what I'm going to say before I say it," he said.

"No, I only know what you are thinking. I don't know what you will say. You speak very little of your mind."

He would try to speak more clearly. "That was so good," he said. It was an effort to say good and not nice. He felt pleased with himself for winning the struggle of discretion and care. She squeezed his elbow. He detached his arm, feeling there might be yellow worms of rheum in the corners of his eyes—lust, tears, dirt—and wiped his eyes with his sleeve and then handed his arm back to her. She took it, laughing at him.

"Nervous," she said, "American."

As they staggered away, wobbly-legged, he glanced back at the dead bird. It was not a dead bird. A child had dropped a brown bag with a peanut butter sandwich, but there were real insects carrying away the sweet glue.

He began to laugh.

She asked: "Why?"

He pointed and said nothing and she couldn't have understood. But she too began to laugh; his relief and pleasure reached her.

"American," she said, "nervous. But so friendly, so nice." She suddenly turned and looked at the dead peanut butter bird. "You know," she said, "when we were there, I thought I saw dead small animal. How long have you known Uwe, my husband? How long have you been married? I want to stretch, I want to run."

She was still excited; she was not at peace, he thought.

"It feels so good, my nervous friend, to make a kind of love! And you don't have breasts!"

He was startled.

"I mean some men your age, in Norway at least but I think in America also, at your age they start to have, oh, what would make a woman be called 'small breasts.'"

He felt proud not to have breasts. It had been a long time since his wife had noticed his virtues.

"On the other hand," she added thoughtfully, in order not to praise a nervous fellow overmuch, "you do not enjoy loveplay so sturdily—you have such word?—so sturdily as you must in the future."

"Or in the past," he said, and believed this must not be a dream, because then he would be grinding his teeth, or a nightmare, because he would be trying to wake from it.

She held his arm more tightly. She read his thoughts before they came to him. "You know nothing about me," she said, "and you wish to know nothing about me." Briskly, lithely, sturdily, she matched her stride to his. She was a skier. That was one thing he knew. In the green air of a city park he could make out the little slicelines of age around her lips which very fair women, skiers, and northern women seem to get in their early thirties. And what signs did she find of his age? Fair ladies always smell sweet; darker gentlemen like himself need to work at it. She had had her nose at his chest, she had moved it away—

"As long as you are content and relax," she said, "I am happy. I am content. I am, you know, poor Lauren, anyway frigid and so hate it when a man pound pound pounds at me, thus this timidness pleases very much—"

"I'd like to please you more."

"Shush, shush, dear. I know, most men do. And maybe you will, why not? I am healthy, you are also—"

"Thank you."

"All this," she said, as if it were the dedication of a memorial, "all this was only for immediate liking. Immediate liking comes to this, I think."

"I like immediate liking," he said.

"Such cravings and impatience and always thinking backwards or forwards," she said. "Today, however, you showed me the ancient ruins of your city and this lovely green place, American."

7

It was late evening, the child was asleep, and tomorrow they would see Paul and Paula and a miracle would occur. When something is important enough, a miracle is supposed to happen. His wife saw that he was looking straight through the front page of the newspaper, which was filled with problems for which there were no miracles, toward the resolution he was dreaming. She was amused and she was also made impatient by futile dreaming. She had a little smile on her face as she stood in the doorway to contribute to his thought. "Am I interrupting?" she asked. "No? Then I'll say something. You used me when we were married to make yourself happy, what you called happy, my dear, and my objection now is you're still using me—"

He woke up rapidly. "Everybody uses everything," he said. "And we're still married."

"—to keep you *un*happy, or what you call unhappy. But

seems like the important thing is how you make me the only thing in your life."

"Our kid. The school. The world."

She shook her head. "Happy or unhappy, it still comes from me. This is what you've got to work out."

"Don't you like being important?"

"Not like this. Makes me unimportant for myself, because I matter so much to you I have no rights for myself. Makes me feel I'm selfish if I stop thinking about Poor Unhappy Husband. Excuse lecture, please, but you do draw the words out of me. I used to have to feel happy just because the big strong lover was so satisfied with himself."

He stared. "You're describing a monster."

"If only! Then I could just walk away without Paul and Paula, without all this jabber! You've got me speeching, too. But you're so generous how you use me, you're so grateful, or then you moon around—"

"You have a strong line about us, don't you?"

"I'm still reacting to you, that's the horrible thing. You're still making me talk when I'd rather say nothing, just live, just *live*, Mister! Oh, horrible is too strong a word, except that's how it feels. I can't escape you. That really is a horror. You're still the person who makes it happen for me."

He said softly, "You're still the person who makes it happen for me."

"Ah!" She raised her arms triumphantly. "The light! You're smart, aren't you? So if we're both so smart, why don't we separate in addition to divorcing?" She was smiling and shone with cleanliness and good health and her eyelids were, it seemed, retracted so that the brightness of blue and white and black iris and pink capillaries filled her face with meat glow. "Isn't that a good idea?" she asked. "To divorce and also to separate and go our own way and not be responsible for each other and free me, free me, *free,* god damn it?"

If she was so happy in her rapid new understanding and exasperation, fulfilled in the control of matters, why was her hand shaking with something she had not yet done or said?

"The important thing is not to get worked up," she said. "So say something easy and not worked up."

"Let's just sit without talking a minute."

"And you'll want me to hold your little hand!" she said, and walked out of the room.

She knew he would follow her. She liked striding this way and that to punctuate her decisions. But when he followed her, as she knew he would, there was another person in the next room. Her eyes were dulled and her head was shaking. A shiver passed back and across her chest. Her head vibrated as if, yes—and her eyes were red, too—as if she were connected with some electric tears short-circuiting, but she didn't cry; she went on speaking: "I realize I started it this time. Listen, you try to understand. Listen to *me* for a change. I'm trying to stay alive, can you figure that? I'm doing things the hard way for you and I know that but for me too it's hard. It's been hard all the way down so don't pity yourself. It was hard before I met you. You married me, so why should it be any better? I always got mean and crazy sometimes, ask my mother. I couldn't stand myself. Now I can stand myself sometimes, that's an improvement, but then I can't stand you, so what's the gain? I just, that's what it mostly is, I'm just lonely and I can't, wasn't made for a pretty little marriage. Food doesn't taste, air doesn't breathe, I haven't got it straight. Life is what I want to divorce, mister. I can't even separate myself from *things.* I don't connect. So I want to disconnect. It's not you and me and the kid—it's the whole everything fucking deal —now you understand?—can't get with you and can't get without you—*do you understand?*"

"No," he said. "I wanted us to make it together."

She smiled. "That's the story of our life, dear. All good things in the past tense." She kissed him very gently on the lips, once, twice, again, just brushing his lips with hers. "Goodnight," she said.

A few minutes later she was sleeping, even snoring a little, like their child after a cold. He was entirely awake, chilled and clenched. He wanted to tell her yes, he understood; why not wake her and tell her that?

But he didn't because she would just find it funny. He hurt and she knew it as much as he knew how she hurt. They needed each other and what else? She was determined to stop all this needing since it had never done her any good.

That's how it is, he thought. Love makes it all happen, so we think, love does impossible work. But she's right, she's right: It doesn't.

Her snores stopped as she turned on her side. She sighed in her sleep. He snuggled against her. It was how their daughter snuggled. Her breathing, as she seemed to swell in long sleeping takes of breath, made her body rise around him like a trembling volcano. He must have been sleeping, too; dreamt of boiling edges, dreamt of lava.

Paul was rubbing his hands together in a wakeup sizzling gesture when they entered. He saw the squeeze bottle of Jergen's Lotion by the table near Paul's chair, which also held the telephone, the telephone answering machine, the tape recorder, the cigarets, the coffee cups (three), each with its little armada of midget brown Marlboro submarines, the ashtray overflowing, the notebook, the appointment pad.

"Dry hands. Interpersonal tension, an occupational disease with a wide range of symptoms," Paul said. "In my case, scaly derma." Paul peered intently at both of them. "You look better," he said with genuine concern. "What's the matter?"

"I look better?"

"Are you Acting Out? You look better, but definitely tired. I'd say, frankly, older. Yet better. There's something here I like and something here I don't like. What is it?"

"You tell me."

Paul shook his finger humorously at them both. "Learning to play games, aren't you? Okay, *you* tell," he said to her.

"Maybe he's found a light of love," she said.

"It's in the cards," Paul said. "Since he didn't go off the Bridge, did he? Did he, Paula?"

"No, he didn't," said Paula grudgingly, evidently on the track of another idea.

"I remember now," Paul said. "She visualized you going off the Bridge, your wife, I mean, not Paula, of course, and she doesn't care. So are you growing?"

"Shrinking," he said.

"Haha. A joke about me, is it? Or can it be weight you're thinking of? Maybe that's what makes you look younger, yet older. Skinny, yet slim. The paradoxes of the human potential is what we have here."

Paula raised her hand. "Sir? Sir?" she asked. "May I speak? Paul, do I sense some hostility toward our client? Do you realize he has hardly spoken today, and she has barely spoken up? I feel, I feel, I feel, Paul, exclusion here. I feel they barely have taken positions. I fccl—"

Paul looked downcast. "You're right. I'll have to ride with that. I'll abide with your epiphany a tad. I was sitting here feeling sorry for myself about my derma problem, how I can't give up smoking, my tobacco tars and resin-soaked anima, and this here couple bears the burden—*but why do they put up with it?* Such must be our question. I have this ethical and emotional question for you. Why was it up to you, Paula, to do the job of gut-level kicking and screaming for this blocked, affectless nonsuicide and his wife who is so intent on growth that she can't live each day as if it might be her last. Desiderata, Baltimore, I think," said Paul. "Not my original thought." He cocked his head to one side, wondering if perhaps it might be more original than he suspected. "Though its application here may be kind of neat, which is why I'm sitting in this chair and not you, and why you are paying, not me."

"A penetrating observation," he said.

"A sarcastic response," Paul said.

"The hour is speeding by on gassamer wings of smalltalk," said the wife.

"Gossamer," said the husband.

"I said gassamer."

"Okay, okay, okay," Paul said. "If you want to get sidetracked in literary discussions, okay, but I feel, and correct me if I'm wrong, Paula, there is a basic problem going down. It's not just what they say it is or think it is or gas off it is. Look how much better that poor grown boy says he feels when last week we were questioning whether or not, and how she would feel, if he took the Bridge route. So to me, Paula, how about you? the issue may go very, very deep."

"It's our marriage that goes deep," he said.

"Paula?" said Paul.

"Well, he stated the problem as he sees it. Maybe we should deal with that."

"I'm dealing, I'm dealing." Paul gave it further thought while he consolidated the fleet of coffee-soaked cigarets from three cups into one. Now he had a storage place for old coffee and cigarets. Two cups were freed for other action. A splash of coffee spilled on his appointment book and very carefully he wiped it with a paper napkin that said *Wendy's* on it. "We're dealing," he murmured.

The husband sneaked a look at the wife. She was sitting with her legs crossed at the ankles. Her shoulder bag hung from the chair. She did not sneak a look at him in return. He stared. She now turned a wide, unblinking gaze at him. There was no expression in it except awake and aware.

Quietly and intelligently she was contained within herself. No sparks were emitted; the fires lay banked inside.

In this silence, the four of them sitting together, something was obliging him to reconsider matters—Paul admitted that thought was not always a bad thing. Was he in love with her because he had suffered for her? Was it really self-punishment, masochism, as she said? Was it because, having given his love to her, he liked how it felt to give love?

Did he also like how it felt when she gave love back?

He remembered stroking her neck and shoulders when she lay abed sick. The memory in his hands and fingertips was more vivid than making love to her. Nursing her when she was pregnant, or when she had the flu, or when she was merely sleepless and lonely. *Wake up, please,* she had asked him, *I'm lonely.* He had waked.

And now all at once he remembered making love to her.

He felt his face turn hot. Paul and Paula had been observing him quietly. Could they read his thoughts? Paula seemed about to speak, but Paul suddenly gave a push to his chair with his hands, propelling his body up and at them. "I detect!" he cried. "A man who says he loves! But his problem goes back much further, and exists parataxically—I'll explain that term—in his very digestion! He's hung up!"

The husband shrugged. He was a little relieved by this speech.

"And you too," Paul said unsparingly to the wife, "in a different way you are struggling with your past!"

"I'll stipulate that," she said.

Paul smiled at her. "How's your love life?" he asked.

She shrugged, but uncrossed her ankles.

"You uncrossed your ankles when you answered me," Paul said.

"I didn't answer you yet," she said. "I was getting ready." She crossed her ankles again. "Working on it," she said.

"We'll get back to you. And yours?" he asked the husband.

"I didn't choose anything or anyone," he said.

"No one asked what you think about it. No one asked you to blame your wife or anyone. One only asked: How's your love life, buddy?"

He wanted to tell his wife the whole sad story of his love of her, his need for her—she was his dearest friend, wasn't she? strong and sure, wasn't she?—as if this feeling, these feelings, were a kind of self-deceit for which she could console him, a sin for which only she could forgive him. He wanted this, and then he remembered her laughter, and then a shiver of loneliness rang through him. He could tell her least of all. Her humor would be high and sharp, but then she would come down to focus on him, to look into his eyes with feeling and sincerity—*you love me, do you?*—and she would say: *That's your problem.*

In fact, intelligently, feelingfully, thoughtfully, considerately, she wouldn't know what in the world he was talking about.

This dearest friend was a stranger and no friend at all. There was no reason to blame her for a natural catastrophe.

"I'm repeating," said Paul. "This is the third time. Wool-gathering is a sign of not being here. So how's your love life, brother?"

He waited, but no one helped. "Working on it," he said finally.

"Then don't play the blame game," Paul said. "That's progress. Even if you're trying to grow as your wife is trying, that could be progress. You may be getting off the dime. Shitting or getting off the pot. Moving and changing."

Time was nearly up.

"We haven't explored the conflict karma this time. I don't want to waste your juice. Dear: are you bored with your husband? Has that changed any?"

"It hasn't changed."

"See, husband?"

He would not weep. He would not rage. He would not reply.

"Well," said Paul, dismissing them, "it was your dime, your hour, yours to waste not or want not, my friend. But worry not, also. Sometimes they're not productive and that can be productive too, for what it reveals. This may have been that."

He was taking the Marlboro butt fleet, harbored in coffee, to the kitchen.

"Sayonara means we'll all be trucking on back to the fray," said Paul.

Paula said softly and warmly, "Try to have an hour alone now. Paul was a little uptight. Try to continue on your own while your irritation is fresh, okay? It'll be productive. I'll be with you in spirit." She lowered her voice. "Your hour was up, so no charge for this insight. I get pissed with him myself." She pulled at her pants, drawing them back over her hips, where they tended to ride low due to professional sitting. She blushed. She decided to take further action. She cupped her hands and called in toward her colleague. "Paul! Am I ever pissed with you!"

There was a momentary pause, and then Paul's cackling laughter returned to them from the john. "Paula, darling," he said, "you're definitely making progress. Would you be able to admit you felt pissed last month?"

The couple walked to their automobile. They had driven here together. They would leave together. Suspicion of family therapists brought them together in a moment of united front. "Paula, I kind of like her," he said.

"You think she's soft on you."

"Maybe. At least she's human. She's trying. She's not out to get me."

"Everybody's human."

"Okay," he said.

"God, the sitter wanted to be home early. Come on, let me drive."

"I'll drive a little faster."

"Do you think, dear, other people are out to get you?"

He considered this problem. "No," he said. "But sometimes I've been wondering if the kid is mine. I don't see how I could be the father of your child and yet you, yet you—"

She took this calmly and rationally. Nothing surprised her anymore. Busy with her own life, she dealt with him like the weather—protect yourself, turn the heat up, accept what comes. She explained: "I'm just tired, dear. I wasn't so tired when we made the kid. Maybe it was a mistake on my part, but I just wasn't tired of you yet." He slowed down. He didn't want an accident. "You see, there's a method in their boring outspokenness. Paul and Paula. I'm outspeaking now, too."

From his cracked heart he uttered the words: "I'm beginning to wish you wouldn't."

"This is one sitter I've lost. It's after five already. Maybe I should let you start telephoning all the high school kids in town. After all, you're the parent, too," she said, "so we can proceed on that line of argument henceforward."

He knew he was wrong. And yet his sinking dread convinced him, and her answer did not, and he longed to take their baby out to examine her jaw, her ears, her navel, her ribcage for what they might tell him. And knew this was insane, of course.

He was also wondering if Paul and Paula had laid on their act for their benefit, and then was surprised to hear his wife answer him, which meant he must have spoken. "I'm not about to add them to my very short list of people I need to figure out," she said. "I'm cutting that list to a minimum. Two maybe."

His heart jumped a beat. So she was interested in him after all.

"Me and my child," she said.

Of course their daughter was his. Yet he was only a father, and he needed the mother to tell him who he was. Someday, on his deathbed, he proposed to discuss how he felt about his wife, and to convince her of its importance, but unfortunately his heart still beat vainly and regularly, his cells multiplied and perished in good order, he sweated from anxiety and exertion and digested his food without undue ruckus. There was no peace in an imminent grave. She was still listening politely, but that was the limit of her attention. "I'm dying!" he said.

"I know it's hard on you," she said. "I'll pay the baby-sitter if you'll go check on the kid."

By the time he finished standing and staring at their sleeping child—the little bubbles of air, the soft plumbing sounds of breathing, the soft fur of lash at the eyes—the baby-sitter had gone and his wife was standing naked at the bathroom door, preparing, he guessed, for a shower. She seemed unaware that she was standing there, thinking, a blotch of hair unshielded, her long graceful arm leaning on the door, a shower cap in her hand. She too had been going over matters.

"It seems," she said, "it just seems like a good idea at the time, which is now."

"Life isn't an idea."

"But this is it. Why must I keep saying all this? You better process it. This is my idea and my life."

"You have perfect teeth even if they're off-color."

"What?"

She looked frightened, as if he might try to hit her in the mouth.

He tried. She slammed the bathroom door shut.

"Suckhole!" she cried. "That concludes the discussion."

8

SHE WAS calling at his office ("Your wife is on the phone, do you wish to speak with her?"). He knew several of her voices. This was the one of certain courting times, girlish and tired, and he had not heard it lately. "Would you like to come home early? It's such a nice fall day, I've got a baby-sitter, I was just going alone to the beach, have a cup of coffee alone—"

"I can get away," he said. "I can arrange it."

There was a slight pause. Sometimes, just before their child was born and just afterwards, when she would call in this voice with this request for company, he would reply with obviously disguised, therefore undisguised irritation: I have a job. I have people who depend on me, I can't just . . . But I'll come home straight from work.

Now he said: "I'll be right there."

Her voice had both laughter and weariness in it: "That could be nice."

Could, he thought, going through a traffic light as it changed, not cautious enough, *Could.* What's that, the conditional subjunctive imperative polite? Why couldn't she, why didn't she just say, That *will* be nice?

She was making sandwiches. It was Indian Summer. Would he think of his Norwegian friend in the park? Well, he was thinking of her, wasn't he? No, not very much.

He played with Cynthia, making her giggle as he floated her about the room, saying: "You're an airplane."

"Airpain," said the child. "Airpain more."

The baby-sitter, temporarily a parent-sitter as well as a baby-sitter, patiently waited through this display: *What a nice daddy, what a good father, what a bore.* He hadn't seen pedal pushers in years. This was a high school dropout but, his wife said, one of the champs of her farflung staff of baby-sitters.

"We'll be back," his wife informed the girl with her little smile of irony, lifted at the left corner of her mouth. "Do you ever worry when the parents go out, they'll never come back and you'll be stuck forever?"

The baby-sitter was working her gum and stopped the bubble mid-pop. She stared at them both with astonished eyes. "No," she said, "I never worry about that. I got worse things."

His wife was laughing and shaking her long hair, silky now from a recent shampooing, a recent rinsing, a recent drying, laughing because she, personally, this young wife and mother, could think of few things worse than having a child to raise. Yet that was what she was doing.

They went out, knowing that Cynthia's brief squall of tears was only a brief squall. She got over it. Even the child wanted her parents to have a chance.

He was shy with her.

She was shy with him.

They drove to the park, and he felt no sense of betrayal because he had taken them to the same park, same corner of the same park, where he had celebrated U.S.-Norway Friendship Afternoon. He knew what he wanted.

"Do you still like this park?" she asked him.

H "Yes, why?"

S "We used to come here. Remember how we used to rent bicycles and you said those narrow hard seats made you think of me?"

H "I said they used to make me think of making love."

S "And I used to say then stand up and pump, don't just sit there coasting—"

H "But you were joking," he said.

S "We did," she said. "Even though we were paying for the bikes by the hour, we made love once in the woods."

H "More than once," he said.

S "Three times," she said, "but the first time was the scariest." And then abruptly she said, "I'm sorry, dearest. I really don't know what I want. I'm scared again. You don't know how scared a person can be."

He put his arms around her.

"You're sad, I know you're sad, I know I make you sad, I'm making you so sad, I see how skinny you're getting, you're just melting away—"

He hugged her as hard as he could. He felt a kind of joy.

"You're sad," she said, "but I don't think you're scared. Not like I am. No, you're not scared the way I am."

He was intelligent enough, he was moved enough, he was lucky enough to say nothing. He was not running a competition with her in Scared and Sad.

At the duck pond he saw a young man, maybe five years younger than himself, with a child a few years older than his, and the young man was pulling pieces of bread out of a paper sack and giving them to the child to throw to the ducks. And he knew, the young man had that bored and dangerously harassed and loving look, he just knew—

As his wife abruptly led him down a more secluded path.

He knew the young man was a divorced father, eking out the visitation afternoon with his child. Later he would be pushing the child on a swing. Still later, in his "condo," he would be wondering whether to take a hot bath and go straight to bed or go to drink in a place with head-banging fern-filled pots suspended all about and ducks quacking louder than the ones in the duck pond.

But maybe, because she had asked him to come to the park with her, alone without their child, he was not to be like that young man. He put his arm around her shoulder and cupped the bone, broad shoulder surprising on slim body, and she did not move from his touch. But after a while, because they were walking down an irregular curved path, it felt uncomfortable for them both and he removed it. He was glad he had done it and she had not protested.

Where were they going here?

What were they doing here?

He stopped suddenly at a blind turn in the path—into a woods, down toward a trickle of stream—and moved her with him; and when she didn't resist, he kissed her. Her fingers crept up his backbone and then lay softly on his neck. She turned her hand lightly on him, as if to warm both sides. "Oh, I'm scared," she said.

"It's more like we're both scared."

"Yes."

"What do you want?"

"I still don't know."

He sighed. He said: "Let us stipulate, as Paul says, let us

stipulate we are both scared and shy. We both have our reasons. We don't know what we want."

Already this was manipulation and lying, wasn't it? He wanted her and she wanted out, even if she wasn't sure that was what she wanted. He knew what he wanted.

"We both have our reasons, I already said that."

She nodded and smiled. "That's all right." Her chilled hand was still trying to toast itself on his neck.

"So let's just be friendly and cuddle."

"Let's go home, can we? I'm sorry I'm being so—I don't know. We can send the sitter out to the park, it's a nice day, babies need air—"

The sitter looked at them with a wrinkled nose—back so soon?—and then still more gloomily when the mother asked her to take the child out. She consented to receive ice-cream money for herself. She observed with no great admiration as the mother tucked clothes on the child, who said to her daddy, "Airpain? airpain?"

He and she looked at the door after it shut as if the sitter and the child might change their minds. Then suddenly her slimness was all over him, she had pushed him to the rug, her narrow tongue was darting into his mouth. "What are you looking for?" he asked.

She laughed ferociously.

"Gently, gently," he said. "We're cuddling."

She took a deep breath. She nestled her head on his shoulder. She reached for him with the hand that seemed to need warming. Then very quickly he began, the shyness gone, and rather quickly, with small nervous squeezings and twitches, tiny tentacular constrictions, she was finished and he was, too.

They lay half-dressed on the carpet, mussed, sticky as adolescents. The fireplace wasn't even lit. It was afternoon. The sitter might get bored and come back earlier than she was supposed to. "You see," he said, "we didn't have to do anything."

"I don't see that at all," she said.

"I mean, because I like you anyway."

"But I wanted to." She decided to ease this into gentleness. "I like you," she said, "and so we did."

What he heard was: And so we did *today.* It was very objective, and as their bodies cooled, the dread of loss returned. He felt like a child, seeing a film he already knew, and it would end, and the doors would open, and an usher would push him blinking out into an alleyway afternoon and the day had gone dead. This lack of courage was not a good way to be with her, especially after their rapid efficient lovemaking—the lovemaking of busy parents—and he would try to hide it; he would try to be different by hiding it; he would really be tougher, he had won something, he could be tougher now. She had called him. She had suggested the afternoon. There was a wetness on the soft slope of her upper arms. And she, here on this rug, in this small adolescent self-absorbed way, had come.

He remembered the disembodied limbs of a mannikin, the thighs of his Norwegian friend in the park. Nothing lived but his wife. And so he got up a few minutes before the sitter returned with the child; he showered; then he played with the child, *airpain, airpain,* while his wife had a long hot bath; and he was sure they would spend the night in each other's arms. He had the child shrieking and exhausted with play by her bedtime. This was not very clever of him. But the child slept anyway, and perhaps this meant she had deeply enjoyed the nervous roller-coaster rollicking with her father.

He did the dishes from their hamburger and salad, their beer, their mini-superette ice cream, their graduate student, young parent supper. She tucked the baby in. She straightened toys. She put a Ravi Shankar record on the stereo. She shrugged; she liked it. She pulled down a corner of the linen on their bed and invited him in without a word. Oh, that was a good idea. The long reverse courtship of break in their marriage had been tumbled with too many words, speculation and debate, too much fret and adrenalin and pituitary and explanations that explained not enough.

Okay. She felt for his crotch and she felt his readiness and that hand which had needed warming now leapt away as if it were scalded. "What!" she cried.

"Surprise," he said.

"My, my. Go, boy, go."

And he thought: Why, she's funny, but she's starved!

But when he went prodding into her, the moisture which received him for a moment in meat confusion clarified itself as if alcohol had been scrubbed over it; he pressed and started to whisper something, nothing, and a dry gate swung shut against him. He was in a hot dry trap.

"Wait," he said. "Patience." He tried not moving. He kissed her cheeks.

"It hurts," she said.

"Wait," he said, "wait, wait."

"It hurts even when you don't move," she said. She wrenched away. "I'm afraid not tonight."

He lay back and said, "Why?"

"I just can't." And she guided his hand. "Feel."

"That can be helped." He began to slide down her body and her arms tightened on him. "I'll help," he said.

"No. Don't."

"Then you can use something."

"No. I don't want to. Evidently I've changed my mind—"

He leaned up on his elbow and looked steadily into her eyes. "Use something. I think it's important."

"I said no. I said, did you hear me? I've changed my mind—

don't!" she cried as he swung on her with his fist, turning his body at the last moment so that his hand pounded into the pillow.

"I won't, don't worry," he said thickly. "I better get out of here. I'll turn the rig off"—Ravi Shankar was still whirling—"and you get your sleep."

He dressed swiftly in the dark. She didn't ask where he was going. He didn't know where he was going. She shut her eyes as if she were sleeping. She was not sleeping. Shoes tied, he stood by their bed. The covers were pulled to her chin. She opened her eyes. She reached for his hand and pulled it to her, and now she was moist and warm, as if he had bloodied her. And she was busy with herself.

"I liked resting in your arms," she said, "but you were pushing me."

He said nothing.

"You want to take back everything all at once."

He said nothing.

"Go," she said. "You have my permission," she said, "find a girl, have fun, fall in love, do what you want, okay?"

She was still working at herself.

"Fuck all you want," she said.

He was out. The shriek of his motor on the quiet street sounded like her cry of joy, but of course he was in control of the machine. He was surprised he didn't feel worse.

9

WHERE THE devil could he go at this hour?

He drove a route that was familiar to him, as if it were morning—across this intersection, onto the one-way, down past the shopping center. There was only one man hurrying on foot through the dark—no, another.

It wasn't as late as it seemed. A slow procession of cars floated through the night, blacks, teenagers, a few women alone on earnest missions, perhaps telephone company employees, and swollen-faced night workers in twill uniforms. It was past the hour when couples like him and her would be coming home from the movies or visiting the in-laws or slightly important meetings. It was past the hour of husbands on errands to the Seven-Eleven shop. The city had laid in its supply of ice and aspirin until morning.

He thought of a friend who might put him up for the night:

I've left my wife . . . Did I awaken you? We've had a fight, but I think this time it's more than a fight—

He had gone to work and married a woman and had a child and let his friends slide away. He wanted no friend to explain to. He wanted her.

Her confusion. Her sadness. Her regret. Her determination. How he admired her. Her mystery. Her coolness. Her shadowed reality. How he remembered her when she was other and different, when her determination was to have him and keep him and please him. How he still loved her.

Why?

This distance and shadow were in himself, too. Boredom with his own need sent him to needing the gentle lady thought to be cool and decisive, the cool and decisive lady thought to be gentle. He no longer knew which from which—so much fuss about a tall woman with blotched skin and upper thighs too heavy for her long legs and an unappeased heart and a kind of grace in her smile.

She was wooing herself again. She would let him win nothing. Yet she had wanted him; and now, for the little she had given him, she was wooing herself all over again, making sure she had given him nothing, it was all still hers; she was willing to show her contempt.

And yet cheeks had been wet with tears.

And there were still tears on her face.

Her closeness to him and grief were only the twitch of dying —a sadness at everything going, time wasted and over. She knew the world moves on.

She was far ahead of him. She was looking everywhere, and she had no shame, and she didn't care who knew. Her high-colored cheeks were flushed. Her body was slim and mobilized. He remembered a blue silk blouse and the flesh cool beneath the silk and why had she thrown out that blouse only because it had gotten old, a little frayed where it pulled out of her velvet pants? His fingers on the cool expanse of skin when he had come home to find her wearing the blue silk blouse he liked, because he liked how it fell from her shoulders and breasts, how her flesh felt to his fingers.

Well, he too had no shame. But he was looking only to her for the dire connection he needed. He still called her wife; she was still whom he craved. He thought, with enraged optimism: Perhaps knowing more, if I save this, if *we* save this, it will be better, it will be more, it will be marriage instead of merely "my wife," "my husband," he, she, they, us. She had been sad. He had touched her. Something had touched them.

Leaving him was not just an idea for her. She meant it. She was really pulling out.

He didn't want things as they had been, or even as he had thought they were. He didn't want this ignorance. He didn't want his own complacency (married, that's it, a child, a job, a wife, nice moments, smoky fireplace and walk on beach, a few expectations, the march of years, all okay and in order).

Her flushed, freckled cheeks were often white with anger. Her distress had made her pale beneath the healthy outdoor American glow. Bravely she thrust the distress deep within, like a bomb, where it had exploded in his face, made fragments of their life, annulled the walks on beach, divorced the smoky fireplace where they used to make love, giggling—murdered the giggling.

She used to become white with anger when she had her period. Little white spots exploded near her mouth. She was dismayed. Her body was using her. She clucked at herself in the mirror; she tried to hide the spots with expensive, useless preparations; he said, It'll pass in three days, you know that, it always does. And she said: But I hate it . . . Now she looked like that all the time.

He had to recalibrate a station which was tuning out under its own power failure. It was switching to alternative power. Her anger had seemed to be merely anger and desire to hurt—alternative power. The shadows of her other man or men. The shadow of her imagination of other men, of freedom, of no one. The deep shade of her icy body huge over him. A creature of nightmare, of control, of monstrous loveliness was hurting him.

And now as he drove aimlessly about the city he saw something else in her. Grief. She had lost her way and blamed him and had lost her own way and wanted not him but another guide. Other women in this grief and confusion wanted other women instead of men, and she might come to that, too. In her dreams, she told him, she became friends with a widow; they each had a child to raise in a kitchen world without men; but she told him she waked with the hope of a man's hairy arms around her, so long as she didn't have to speak with him or know his name. ("No, I can't go to fern bars and find one, I just can't do it," she said.) Her adventures were limited by shame and she despised it. She could not find familiar women; she could not find strange men. She was in mourning for something; for what she had felt for him; for something gone before they had met.

Her hands had been praying for something under the damp sheet in the glowing tropical wetness of her body.

He loved her. He wanted her happiness (only hers could save his own). He was thankful for his loved one's misery. He was impure. Like a bureaucrat, like a principal with a school board, he waited for the mechanism to play out and rescue him. He was stupid and cunning and put all his desire where it helped neither him nor her.

"Don't worry," she had said.

"About what?"

"I think I'm getting my period. You don't start a new romance with a period coming on."

"I don't," he said, "but I would."

"I don't," she said, "period, full stop."

Then she looked like a child, tucked in, tucked under blankies, ready for sleep, the day's heat shifting into the night's heat. They smiled at each other. He remembered his shame when he found a stain on his underwear while they were undressing together during the good times. He imagined her distress now; he could not imagine her distress; she was smiling like a child; she was sad and lonely like a child.

Her coldness was not aloofness. Her indifference was not uncaring. Her irritability was not bad temper.

She did not know how to reckon with her own sadness. Nothing in early feeling had prepared her. Loss had been left out of the accounts.

This sadness changed nothing for them. It helped him not at all. It only reminded him of her need, of his hopes and weakness, and how once she had needed him and he believed she would not stop.

Her anger was the ice in which she stored heat, like an Eskimo's igloo. Her indifference was what she did with love. It was her depth turned inside out.

Oh, confusion. How could they let this loss happen to them?

A two-color Pontiac station wagon with high-rider undercarriage pulled alongside at a light. A man in a stocking cap on the passenger side saw his eyes flick toward him and began a ballet of staring, staring, head twisted to the side, nose squashed against the window, jerking up and down and upside down, in mechanical marionette movements, turning this way and that— traffic was moving now—while the driver kept in the parallel lane, not letting him free.

He screeched around a corner and escaped them.

There's madness everywhere, not only mine, he thought.

He realized where he was finally driving the little car with the sleeping bag in the trunk. He was spending the night in a sleeping bag in his office. He was not going to tell a friend. He was not going to a hotel. He would not telephone Miss Oslo even if she had no husband. He was planning to curl up on a floor which smelled of chalk and green cleaning chemicals. There was a rug near his desk. He had his own bathroom. He liked sleeping on the floor in hot weather. He could say it was hot weather. Everything was still temporary.

He drove into the empty, oil-gleaming parking lot. PRIVATE. Reserved for the Ass't Principal. He maneuvered into his space in an empty field of asphalt, not a single car there, the only interruption to the expanse of shiny black a single tree which the planners had decided not to move when they had expanded the lot. He called it the Ecology Tree. His wife had laughed.

He had left his office early. There would be papers on his desk, and a little stack of pink telephone slips. He admitted himself with his own key. The night cleaners had gone. The smell of green floor cleaner was strong. He felt his eyes turn restless, and felt the pain behind his left eye, where surely, if he lived long enough, his first stroke would clap him down. Lightning through the congested bulge of bone, optic nerve, and brain would make him null. Not yet. Not ready yet, dear one.

Murk in that bulge. Eyes filled with tears. Glad not to be driving anymore. He toted his blue down bag.

His fist in the pillow had caught one of her hairs and it was stuck between his fingers. How long had his fist been clenched? He drew out the long reddish, fairish hair—he sniffed, one hair has no smell—and then watched it drift like a spider's filament to the floor.

He unfolded his sleeping bag. The cord let go when he pulled the knot. That's always nice.

A black ant with a large shiny segmented body was speeding

across the floor. If it meant to carry away his wife's single strand of hair, it might still need help from its mates.

What power and powerlessness in nature.

He was not sleepy. He sat in his underwear in his pale wooden Metropolitan School District swivel chair and dialed. Her sleepy voice answered, "Hello? Hello? Hello?"

If she said his name, he would speak.

"Hello? Hello?"

He replaced the phone.

He said to her: "We would never have been friends if we hadn't become lovers. We never would have married if you hadn't wanted it. And now it's too late to turn back. Please."

But he had already hung up when he said this and in their house she would be wondering if it was he who had called and said nothing, a breather he was becoming, if she woke enough to wonder anything at all.

I beg you, I beg you, dearest.

10

HER ARIAS filled the air when she chose to sing forth rage. His own filled his head, boiling like the center of the earth. When she strode back and forth in the kitchen, he admired the opera while he thought of war, murder, desertion, fatal accident, anything which could take him away from her, her away from him. Marriage is a bond, he thought.

He had a job, a child, and a wife, and he could not quit them, and she sang, her heels clattering on the kitchen floor. Usually in the kitchen she kicked off her shoes, but now she wore them for greater hardness.

"I bet I've found a lover," she said.

"You're the best judge of that," he said, leaning against the sink, a dish towel in his hands, as if ready to dry off and polish her labors, whatever they might turn out to be. Wet forks gleamed in the tray. Should he take a pot and begin scrubbing while she told him about her lover?

But it was she who was scrubbing, speeded with spite, and crying out, "I just wanted to get away, I don't care what you do or did or didn't do or did with that girl—"

Does she know? he thought. And what girl? He almost remembered a woman in a park, Scandinavian she was, and he began jangling a handful of forks in the towel. One fell. He didn't laugh.

"I'll give you credit!" she sang. "You're not a total disaster. You got promoted. The school system gives you an A. You get your ass on television and in the PTA bulletin, telling parents how to control adolescent acne or agony or whatever it is. You look at your face and you don't ask where mine is, but *I* ask. I want to know where I am. I have to worry about what I say about you to others, but thank God I don't have to worry what I say to you."

"Say it," he said.

"I'm saying it!"

"Do I have to listen to this?"

"It's your choice. You're still here. Maybe you do."

And he didn't use a fork on her. He didn't slam past her and into car again. He said, "Shhh, the child," and waited for more.

"I'm sick of being Mrs. Principal, the Young Educator's Wife. I'm sick of getting invitations to your friends' houses. I'm sick of finishing your laundry and your finishing my sentences. I'm sick of people looking at you and I'm just there, nobody—"

People look at you because you're lovely, he thought. I do. You're very colorful, my dear, he thought.

"Do you thank me for doing your shirts? That would be worse if you thank me!"

"I do," he said.

"It's worse!"

She was covering lots of ground in the kitchen, miles maybe, back and forth, putting things away, taking them out, not finishing.

"Sure you help out, you started to when you got scared of me. You play with the kid. I think you even like the kid. I even admit you like me a little. But it would take twenty years to catch up with what you owe me, and you haven't got twenty years—"

He dropped the forks. It was like dropping a child's toy piano. "That's enough. That's enough," he said.

"Why listen? Why are you listening? I can talk to myself, as I usually do. But for some reason you're willing to listen." She went on without waiting for him either to interrupt or not to interrupt. There was a little gleamy rain of forks on the floor, not one of them covered with blood. "Maybe you have a girlfriend, so you're impervious to anything I say, anyway."

Maybe she has a lover and maybe I have a girlfriend, he thought. Who knows? Who cares? He could stoop and pick up a fork and bury the prongs in her breast. He could stoop and pick up a fork and bury the prongs in his stomach. He could go on listening and hear her out.

He could pull the cans and dishes out of the wall. He could pull the house down around them.

He could do nothing.

He said: "I try—do you really think I don't care?"

Her laughter peeled out, crazy and forlorn. "Poor baby, poor baby, he *tries.*"

She put her arms around him. They kissed and staggered together in the kitchen. When she announces she hates me, he thought, we make love afterward. Is that why I let this go on?

They made love politely in their bed, both of them smelling of fight and fatigue. Sleep. Sleep. Her breathing was steady, profound, and peaceful. He lay there in the wrenched smell of fright and dread; and thought about how lovemaking doesn't necessarily bring love or even sleep. And then something new:

He was going dead on abuse. Love was not love and hatred was not hatred, but numbness was numbness. She doesn't love me? Okay, I've heard that story. She's eager for her freedom? That one, too. There must be other news in the world. Russians, Africans, Cubans, Americans, aren't they doing something else?

Maybe she should take her freedom, my wife, he thought. The darkness lent him this uneasy, insomniac indifference. After lovemaking, he did not dread the thought of her in another's arms. It was only a rumor. He did not dread losing the woman whose tender, brilliant, hilarious smile had delighted him when she was the mysterious creature he craved and that wasn't so long ago, either.

I'm a worthless husband? Let her leave me.

She has established I'm worthless to her? Let me get out.

She was icy and hot, she was creamy and soft, she fell into sleep like a child.

He was sad.

She said sleepily, "Dear?"

"I'll be okay," he said. "I'll just get a little air."

Worried, still in her doze, she said: "Dear?"

"Go to sleep. Go to sleep."

It was not a lullaby he was singing to her. Fire was creeping along his roots. But as he lay there in the dark, looking out at the dark, there was nothing to burn but himself.

Finally he too slept. He dreamt about laundry and forks and child's mess to be washed. It's hard to be a woman. In his sleep, he pitied himself; in his sleep, he thought how odd to dream himself into being the woman he loved.

Waking, a school bureaucrat's normal routines did not stop. They had to continue for a while the life they had made. He thought her willingness to wait meant something more than it meant.

They drove to a dinner party in station-wagon suburban country. White colonial garage with Ranchwagon there parked. (Is this what's wrong? he wondered. Something basic like this?) It was a couple they liked and never thought about when they weren't in sight of them. Before dinner, with drinks, he did not sit with her on the couch because he knew she did not want him touching her, his thigh near hers warming it, his breath mingling with hers when they turned, as couples do, to smile upon each other. He sat in a chair across the room, smiling at her sometimes, and looked at her with puzzlement, his stomach churning. He wished they could have told their friends about their troubles. He wished everybody could be honest with everybody. He wished she loved him still.

On the way home she said, "How like you to take the only comfortable chair in the room."

"How like you recently—"

"To nag," she finished for him.

"You don't know what's in my head. But you're right, I was thinking this is getting—"

"Monotonous," she finished for him.

The motor hummed steadily and soothingly.

"I have to survive somehow," she said at last. "I know I don't know how. I'm so angry with you!"

The good sense to say nothing.

"Nothing has any value," she said, "while you're in the way. I shouldn't have to destroy you, should I, darling? But wives do kill husbands, don't they?"

"And husbands kill wives," he said.

They had a chuckle together. It was like friendly old times as they thought about the desire to kill each other.

"Too bad we're not simpler folks. We could go back to Paul and Paula," he said.

"Not that!" she cried happily. "But it was almost fun, wasn't it? It would have been for me. Her *pants*. And he sloshed around and smelled like an old dog. And we even gave them money! But you can't do Paul and Paula alone, can you? It took the two of us to handle them."

They drove back into the city through the late Sunday streets, headlights and streetlamps and silence after their laughter. Neither spoke. It was like sleepy drives home when they were children.

And the baby was crying when they got home, and the babysitter was chewing her gum and saying, "I don't know. I put on the teevee"—a late night horror movie it was, monsters with screws in their gummy foreheads and hairy paws—"but she just said where were you, where were you. I was kind of wondering myself. Tomorrow's a school day."

They paid her off. She wasn't the best sitter, but she lived down the street. He held the child and said, "Screw it, let's play airplane," and he flew her around the room till she stopped crying. Then he said, "Now we'll play dirigible, you'll float so gentle, so gently," and he calmed her, cuddled her, floated with her, danced with her.

"Dance," said the child.

"That's right, that's right, honey," he said.

He felt stained by the shame of another thought besides wanting everything right for their child. He wanted his wife to see how important he was for the child. He wanted her to appreciate him. The Acting Principal was a little boy.

"Put her to bed," she said. "It's late." Then she considered them both. "You're a good father," she said. He smiled. He was happy. He had won a point. "Even if I'm not around, you can handle things."

She was sprinkling gasoline everywhere. He willed himself not to strike the match. She added, "I mean that in the best possible way."

The child was at peace now. Daddy and Mommy were home. He put her to bed, thinking how it would be to handle such things with a housekeeper during school hours, himself the rest of the day. The milk-warm smell of child made him think: Not too bad, rather nice, I love her so. But also impossible, he thought, not sure why this should be so.

When he returned, she was in a robe and nothing else and the robe was not tied. "Come on, come on, come on," she said urgently, "this is a funny time in my life, I want it now, come on, take advantage of it while you can—"

"Shut up!" he cried, the flames shooting up. "Shut up talking like that!"

"Shush, I'm sorry, darling, it just turns me on to talk like that. Let me turn myself on, okay? Even if I want to say dirty things?" She had fallen in love with him; she was wearing a garter belt the first time they met; she took it off and threw it at him, laughing when he tried to undress her. She had undressed him successfully. She had fallen in love; she had climbed out of love.

He would like to recommend another course of action to her. He would like to commend to her the possibility of falling in love with him again. Such, of course, does not happen. It's a one-time-only offer, he thought like a radio announcer, so take advantage of it now. Had he? Had *he*? Had he taken full advantage of the offer while it was still valid?

"Wanna hold my hand?" she asked, standing huge and nude. The robe was spilling down her body. He took her hand. He felt all burdens lifted. A moment ago he might have taken her violently here on the floor. Now he led her to their bedroom, holding her hand.

They made love gently. Oh, he was grateful for this abrupt, silent, and wistful lovemaking. He lay by her side, feeling content and not thinking at all.

She woke him again with words. "Very nice. But I hope

you're not going to make anything of this. I just can't stand your sadness, that expression on your face, there it is again, you're getting so skinny—look!" She pinched him gently. "I just want to make you feel better sometimes. I don't feel, um, desire for you, but it's not that. I don't feel desire for anything. I don't feel it! But I'm confident I will." She grew exasperated at this confidential chat. "I'm getting caught again in your trap of talking and explaining. You think when I don't say anything I'm holding back. And when I speak it's to hurt you. How can I come out ahead? I can't. I've said it all. I have nothing new to say."

"That was so nice a moment ago," he said.

"It was, it was," she said, "what does that have to do with it? I'm not going to fall into that trap. You see, I'm trying to tell you. It's not personal. I feel for you, too, but I just have to be . . ."

"Hard," he said.

"Strong," she said, "stronger."

With his hand he removed the sticky small thing from where it touched her thigh.

"Thanks," she said. "We don't want to be glued together, do we? Men think that pleases me. They're wrong. Free is what pleases me now."

He just murmured, as if it were a good-by in sleep: "Then why don't you just get free? What's stopping you?"

She pulled away. His mood altered like this after they made love. The convulsion leaked his feeling out with the sperm and fluid. "Ach!" she said. She sat up and shook out her hair. "Good, good! I'm going out. I'm meeting a friend. Now that you got what you want, arrange for our kid in the morning."

"*What?*" He sat up abruptly.

She began to laugh. "Just practicing. It's going to come to that soon, isn't it"?

"Oh, God," he said, "are you crazy?"

"No," she said very seriously. "You think I'm playing. You think I'm nuts. You think I'm wild. You're wrong. I think of you all the time. I can't seem to feel anything but anger, and then I just can't stand your sadness, and I don't want to, can't bear, how could anyone? to be married so tight."

11

"LET'S HAVE the happy Sunday of the bereft young men," said his friend Curt, whose marriage had broken up.

"Yes, if it's a nice day let's make a picnic for our kids."

"I'll do the drinks and desserts, you do the food," said Curt. "No, tell you what. You're too new in the game to be responsible for anything. I'll do all the food. Just concentrate on picking me up in your car. That isn't beyond your capacities, is it? You're safe behind the wheel, aren't you?"

"There's a fanatic safe driver here."

"Then what are you complaining about? You can't be insane with grief. Personally, there were months when I didn't trust myself on the highway." He laughed. "I still drive kind of recklessly. It'll be fun to be among the lads again, won't it, pal? Won't we have lots of fun?"

Curt's eyes, the eyes of this old friend, wavered and turned unreliable as they met his. There was a spiteful look as he turned away, and yet he knew Curt wished him well—it was pain that made him keep the spark from passing between them. He wondered if his own eyes had taken on this mean glaze, the skin of his own chin creeping a little with sudden loss of weight, his cheeks yellowing. They both had grown thin; diminished, not slender.

It wasn't a question of right or wrong in their lives. There was no right.

He knew, of course, that his passion for his wife was an attachment to an idea about himself.

Curt's mean evasive eyes said the same thing: I'm nothing without her, buddy. How is that possible, big strong me?

"Plus we'll be good baby-sitters," Curt said.

It was a time of epidemic quarrel, separation, divorce. Like birth, death, and marriage, this was probably always going on, but when it happened to him and his friends, he noticed it better. Curt felt it was the age, politics, feminism—time for the wives to try solving life's problems in another way, since the men only made mistakes. He felt it was his own wife: time for her to solve her own problems in another way. Both secretly felt it was all their fault, each his personal fault, because they were not perfect, as their wives had once seemed to believe they were, as they had intended to be. They would make everything up to their children by being delightful and devoted fathers.

On this Saturday, when he and Curt took their children on a picnic, he told his wife: Do what you want, I'll keep her. . . . There was a certain thrill in visiting the same park where he had bundled with that Norwegian woman, what was her name, the lady with whom he bundled, who was nice to him when he needed someone to be nice to him, before he was ready to be nice enough in return, while he still loved only his wife. He might or might not tell Curt. Surely Curt had a similar boyish adventure to recount, eyes bright for the triumph, corners of mouth slightly downturned with the snickering boyishness of it and the certainty that it did not mean the marvelous things it seemed to mean in the telling.

There are accidents of nearness and need in falling in love, and similar accidents in friendship. Curt's boy was the same age as his daughter, and in a year or so a boy and a girl might not like to play together. Still later they might like to play together a lot. Right now, they were young enough not to care. Curt had a wife who had left him. He had a child. He was morose and ironic. In common destitution, the two men picnicked together with their children like friends and lovers.

"I've been to this park before," he said.

"Who hasn't?" Curt said.

The sun struck through the branches. He remembered a pattern of leaves on the ground—couldn't have.

He decided to tell about his Norwegian lady when it came up naturally. The kids were in the sandbox. The two fathers sat on a wooden ledge, peeling off splinters. We're male mothers, aren't we? . . . No, it's Saturday, you're only a male mother if you do this during working days. . . . Is this getting to know our children?

"This is getting to know each other," he said.

Curt laughed and slapped him on the back. "What a time!"

"It's a nice day," he said, "but you mean this part of the century."

"You got me," Curt said.

"It got us both," he said.

The children were heaving globs of sand at each other. Would a proper male mother say Stop, or would he wait until someone cried, an eye got sand in it? They measured the dimensions of the problem without coming to a statesmanlike answer. An eye got sand in it. A child cried. Two fathers consoled. One of them said, "Stop throwing sand," and the other concurred in this proposal. Temporarily the children stopped throwing globs of wet sand at each other. On an experimental basis one tried kicking a cloud of dry sand, but didn't possess the technology to reach his adversary's eyes. "Nice kids," Curt said, "and whatever happens, at least we've got that."

"Amen," he said.

"Also, we've got the support payments until we're well into late middle-age."

"I said amen. I'm glad. Children are animals, but they're all that matters."

"Not at all," said Curt, "that's going too far, my friend. That's maudlin."

"I'm still glad," he said. "Also I'm not as far along as you are, Curt."

"Yet," said Curt. "But get ready, pal."

They watched over the children with the absently contemplative stare of men lighting their pipes and wondering if they would stay lit. They sighed. They would stay lit.

After awhile, he asked Curt: "You got a friend?"

Curt went on sighing. "Sort of. Yes. No. You?"

"The same thing. No."

"Jesus Christ. Whatever happened to the big fuckers? What kind of a world is this?"

"I don't think we should blame it on the whole universe," he said. "To me, it feels like my fault. My wife's fault. I guess the times contribute."

"Damn right. Without lib—the Women's Movement, yucch!—this wouldn't happen. They dream of liberation and we dream of everlasting love. Isn't that the shits?"

"That was my dream, too. It hurts."

They studied their children. It was like reading and rereading the back of the cereal box. It was the thing they did to put brain waves at rest. The two children now tried peaceful play. They were digging. They were patting towers together. They had found a pink plastic bucket. With this equipment in hand, they worked out a project. Grimy palms broke roads through the sand. Curt's child was biting his lower lip. It was a habit of Curt's also. He looked at this friend and shook his head.

"I know," Curt said, "it's worse'n a toothache to lose a wife. I'm not hungry yet, are you? Should we share? I bet you made peanut butter and jelly for your kid, too."

"That's what they like best. The fancy stuff leaves them cold."

"Toothache," Curt said.

"You want to kill the pain," he said.

"I'm doing it," Curt said spitefully, as if this were a form of bullying. "I'm giving myself a root canal job."

"Yes, and it'll kill love also," he said.

"If love is a form of masochism," Curt said, "and I think it is, that might well happen. I hope so."

"I don't know if I hope so," he said. "I'd like to end the feeling bad. I'd like to feel better."

Curt orated fervently, raising one finger, a pitchman selling a cure on the corner: "Then kill the pain, my friend!" And put his hand down, looked at the finger, put it in his mouth to suck it. "Shall we dine? I brought the sports section of yesterday's paper as a tablecloth, I brought beer for the relatively grownup us and orange juice for the little ones, I suggest we exchange peanut butter and jelly sandwiches—kids always like somebody else's sandwich better. Who's your girlfriend?"

"Not really," he said. "Norwegian. Married. I haven't seen her in a week or two. Or a month. Not really."

"Whipping it up, aren't you?" Curt asked.

"Let's eat."

They called the kids and they ate. He had brought coffee in

a thermos, half milk and half coffee steaming out of the jug, and it tasted good. The sun on leaves. Lacey shadows. A pal to make rue with. Life isn't so bad, is it? With a pal? With Norwegian women turning up now and then? The euphoria he sometimes felt when the coffee hit the right nerves: I'm alive, I'll stay alive, I have a chance to survive.

When he felt good, he felt pugnacious. It was self-pity turned inside out. And when he felt rotten, the fight went out of him. Curt grinned and touched his arm. He too had these sudden rises and dizzying falls of the uprooted man. "We're just holding on, and They want something new," Curt said. "Mine has a Group."

"Not mine," he said. "Mine is an individual operator."

"Who's to say what the modus operandi of women is anymore?" Curt asked. "What are their plans?"

He looked at Curt on the bench with their children oozing peanut butter in the sandbox and said: "I didn't plan my life. I lived it. A woman appeared. I must have needed love. I loved her. Life seemed organized. A child. The days."

"I hear you," said Curt.

"Now I'm losing the wife."

"But it's not just starting over, is it?" asked Curt.

I lost her! I lost her! he thought.

Curt was telling him the same story. "It's the Horsewomen of the Apocalypse," he was saying. "When our kids are older, we can toss balls around on Visitation Day. Hey! You're not listening! You're supposed to say our balls are getting tossed around already."

"I think I've lost her, Curt," he said. "I don't think I have a chance."

12

SHE HAD taken a lover.

A churning in the belly. A dizzy disconnection of eyesight, hearing, touch, smell, as with a fever. A fever. Things were there and yet they were not there. A taste of yesterday's sardines in his mouth; he had not eaten sardines yesterday. A clap of heartbeat when he thought of the rest of his life, an extra thump he didn't need. His toes were not straight; his feet did not touch the earth properly. He urinated frequently. He sat groaning on the toilet. His mouth was dry. He drank more water. His hands were dry. His ear rang with a telephone summons. No one there. His throat felt constricted and his breath seemed to whistle through it. Was that the noise? He breathed through his nose and his breath whistled through it. A nerve on his eyelid twitched. When he looked in the mirror, feeling the twitch, he could not see it. Then he looked again and saw it—a tiny antrun across his eyelid. His razor nicks hurt. One became infected. With a knife he opened it to drain it and he would surely have a scar. His teeth felt the strain of his dreams. He woke up with a toothache. He felt cold and hot in his mouth with no sense to it.

Some men with the bad habit of grinding nightmares wore rubber bits in their mouths to protect their jaws and teeth. He did not want to wear a rubber bit.

I'm going through the normal difficulties, he thought.

He thought: It seems I'm preoccupied with myself.

He wished yesterday's sardine taste would go away.

The right kiss would make everything sweet, wouldn't it?

She had taken a lover. No doubt his wife now had a lover. If she told him or she didn't, she did. He thought he smelled semen on her fingertips—maybe it was only paprika from cooking, or some other spice he didn't know about—but he smelled her lover everywhere. Her clothes in the little bag she used for laundry. Her hair. He smelled him everywhere. His own stomach threw her lover up at him and made him gag.

"Why are you lurking, lurking?" she asked.

"Nothing to do. Don't feel well."

"Go play with the kid. Stop thinking about yourself."

"I'm thinking about you."

"Then *I'd* like to play with her," she said, and moved toward the nursery room.

He pushed by her. "No, no, let me, you're right, I want to hug her."

He rolled on the floor with the child, making her too excited, so that she laughed until she cried, and her tears mingled with his. His wife, the mother, was washing the paprika off her fingers. The fast-paced life of a modern woman. He stopped rolling and tugging and clutched his child and just hugged her silently and then looked up and the large round unpigmented blue of her eyes was steadily, like the sky, regarding him. She was very quiet now. She almost recognized that her father was sad.

He tried to remember that girl, Sigrid, that pretty girl his Norwegian friend had married. Not Sigrid, Lauren.

He thought of his wife.

He held his child and thought of her.

He thought of his wife.

He was still thinking very much too much about himself.

He sat up and leaned against the wall with his quiet daughter in his lap, in his arms, and tried to think of himself as some Fast-Fucking Fred, an Interesting Person, but it came out: No, Sad-Eyed Dan, the Betrayed Lad whose wife, maybe from cooking, had paprika on her fingertips.

He curled up on a bed with his daughter and played with her lips. She giggled. He put his fingers in her mouth. She licked and sucked. She closed her eyes. Her smile knew everything. She slept. The radiator was turned on too high. He should get off the bed and turn it down. The walls. The ceiling. The heat. He dozed.

A dazed film of himself with odd, tight-fitting Italian clothes and a revolver in his hand, on a street corner, waiting for a man to emerge from a doorway—

A dream of himself as a high school principal, promoted young, interestingly young for the job eight years ago, but wearing any kind of clothes that came along and no revolver at all and just hoping to come home after work to his wife—

The child was sleeping. He slipped his arms from around her and gently rolled her in the quilt. He heard his wife in the kitchen and he went to her. He remembered to look at her. People like to matter to others and people like to know they matter. Her lover could give her nothing but risk and danger and he could still give her everything else. He would not think about giving her the danger of losing him. He did not feel sure enough of himself. But he could give her what he wanted from her. Love. He wondered if she would think him ridiculous if he touched her at some forbidden place. Probably she would move away. Or not move, but laugh. He pressed his fingers against her ass.

"Oh," she said, "it's you. Did you leave the kid on our bed?"

"She's sleeping. I guess I put her to sleep."

His hand just rested there. It didn't pinch.

"Let's just hope she doesn't wet. If she does, it's your mess."

I'm thinking about myself. She's thinking about the danger to our blanket, quilt, and sheets if the kid wets the bed. She's the intelligent one.

"Why are you kissing my hand? Now you're kissing my hand. What is this?"

He bowed. He would make a joke, like an easy lover. "Maybe I'm turning courtly," he said.

"You're turning crazy. We've got to work this out somehow."

"Agreed," he said. "I'm going crazy and we have to work this out."

"I'm trying to be straight with you without necessarily hurting your feelings. That's my intention," she said. "I'm in the woods, too."

"You have your dreams, too," he said. "But what is making me crazy? My heart is pounding like to explode."

Would she suggest a checkup? At the beginning of middle-age, a man should begin to have frequent checkups, especially if his heart tends to pound like to explode.

"Why are you still holding my hand?" she asked.

"I guess I'm still turning courtly in my old age."

"You're turning me off. You're holding too tight. You're hurting. I can't put dishes away with one hand. For a trick, why don't you try it?"

"I think you're right," he said. He let go. "What is making

me so crazy? What could it be? I feel so hurt."

"Hurt, you say? Are you in love? What hurts you? Should you get your annual physical?"

"Which I've never annually got. Dear, nothing is real without you. Dear, your sarcasm is so cruel. What are you trying to do? What are you so succeeding in doing?"

She gazed at him severely. His remark, slipped like sandwich filling between complaint and complaint, that nothing was real without her, seemed to give her some trouble. "You credit me with understanding what I'm doing," she said. "I don't even know what I need—*what is this about my fingers?* Why are you looking at my fingers? Okay: to answer your question if I can: I can't answer all your questions. I see it's a hard time for you. But I'm just trying to find my own questions and maybe one answer in three."

"Your meaning's not clear."

"That's all we can expect. Unclear meanings. That's the whole point. Aren't you smart? You used to be. I used to think you were smarter than me. Wifey leans on smart husband. But now I don't. Live with it, please, okay?"

He wished to be elsewhere, he wished to be another. He was cold and burning with jealousy, with desire. He hated and loved her. He burrowed into himself and wanted nothing more than to escape himself. Then why did his aimless eye suddenly find a grease spot on the wall near the stove? What did careless frying have to do with their lives. Who fried around here anyway? Why couldn't he come to a focus?

His heart would break his chest.

No. His heart would only break itself.

She didn't want to tell him she had a lover. She only wanted him to know it.

"Do you have a lover?" he asked.

"Don't ask stupid questions."

"Do you have a lover?"

"I think we discussed this matter already."

"Do you have a lover?"

She looked at him with her eyes flooded. "I'm just as unhappy as you are," she said. She reached out to touch the walls. She did not reach out to touch him. "I wish we could help each other. I wish I could help myself. I wish someone could help me."

He looked at her hands. The fingers were interlaced and twisting.

"I'm going to get that kid off our bed before she wets," she said.

13

AT WORK, he waited for her to call and ask to meet him for lunch. At home, he waited for her to move to his chair and sit on the arm. He waited for her to smile and say she had had a revelation, a miracle, and everything would be different.

She didn't say that.

He rented the first place he saw near his school. It was partly furnished. It smelled of part-time people and temporary passage, of dust and mice and excess heating. He did not want comfort; he wanted something that meant temporary, for a moment or two, while things fell into place. It was a plus that it cost so little. It was a minus that gradually he found himself leaving clothes there and she insisted on giving him a few kitchen things.

One day he found himself cleaning and scrubbing. Even a temporary nest shouldn't make a fellow sneeze.

But he was just passing through.

I feel awful. This is not tragic. No dignity. I probably smell.
I can't lick myself clean like a cat.

I need a cat. (He laughed aloud.) Or a bar of soap.

He called to say he would take their child out to the, oh,
museum or park or for an ice cream. He just wanted to hear her
voice. "Okay, good," she said.

"I'll see you right now," he said.

"Right now? You're at work."

"In a few minutes."

"In two minutes?"

"What's the matter?"

"Kind of—" Busy? "—thinking."

"I'll be there."

"You'll be here?"

He hung up, shaking. The earth had tilted and everything was
rolling away. Why did he want to hear her voice? His wife was
going. Meaning had gone. Questions asked nothing. The voice
was absent. He put his head in his hands and cupped his throbbing eye with his palm.

He drove home with one eye squeezed shut. He drove slowly
and safely. He believed he drove better than when he was a
contented husband. He remembered taking chances. Now he
took none. He took nothing. When he got there, he sat in the
car a moment. His eye hurt. He still wanted to hear her voice.
He had to ring to get in because she had locked the door from
the inside. He was rattling his key in the lock, near to twisting
and breaking it off, a broken key stuck in the lock, when she
finally answered. She looked flustered. "I'm sorry," she said.

"Were you on the phone?"

"I'm sorry," she repeated.

"Where's the kid?"

"Still asleep. Her nap. I forgot to get her up for you."

"Is there someone else here?"

"Someone else here?"

"Shit! Where are you?"

"Oh, dear," she said. "Sit down."

He did so.

"I've been thinking. Darling, I'm trying to get it straight. I'm going to try to tell you. You know I've been dreaming. Maybe I've found a prince, maybe not. Maybe you are my prince."

"Maybe not," he said in a whisper.

"Okay. Say I'm cold. Okay. Say when you do me like you do, you know, rubbing how you do, I think of the man I might truly love, who wouldn't—who would only need to look at me—who might be my prince."

"Say."

"So I mean, this crisis, I mean it's so stupid."

"Say."

"If we come together again," she asked, "will you love me anyway?"

"How can you ask me that now?"

"I need to know."

He looked at her with all his desire. His eyes were blank; only fear looking out at her; she turned away. "I'm doing my best to rip you out," he said. "If I succeed—no. *When* I succeed. When I succeed, you will be gone for me. You will be dead for me."

She said numbly, "I hope you don't succeed."

"How can you tell me that?"

"I want something else, I don't want you, that's true, but I can only imagine us together. That's true, too. I see us together, oh, in a cabin, not now, later, maybe years from now—"

"How old are we?" he asked. "In this vision of yours, are we grandparents with separate grandchildren?"

"I don't know. I don't plan. I only see," she said. "I might not be rational, making sense, but I've always had to be rational.

Now it's my turn to be normal."

"And in the meantime," he said, "for me—"

"I guess I'm checking out."

She had sad eyes. Those who speak of love, he thought, usually have sad eyes. Or infatuated eyes that dart about with bright wet glintings. Those are also sad eyes. He supposed his own were hooded and sad. The eye that hurt ached as if something was torn in there.

"We don't have ways to say good-by," she said. "I mean women like me. Try to understand. We don't, at least *I* don't run away. I try, but I can't. I'm not an angel, though, in case you thought otherwise. You used to have funny ideas about me when you loved me—" *I still do.* "Dear, I'm trying to check out."

They had talked a great deal and it had done no good. Yet he was glad they were talking. "I suppose you're trying not to hurt me," he said.

"Not particularly trying, as you may have noticed. But I'd prefer not to. Don't want to hurt. Wish I were cozy. But I have my own hurts, dear." Her eyes reddened at the lids; pinkened, rather. They remained dry.

He stared hard into those eyes. The pain behind his left eye was part of him; it was part of the stare. He wanted to force her to feel it. By looking at her, making her see his eyes, sorrow, panic, he wanted to oblige her tears to come.

She recognized it was a contest. She was determined to win. The pink gradually faded; he imagined capillaries opening and pumping; he imagined the heart distantly thrumming; her body was calling itself to order. She winked.

"The kid's asleep," she said. "You could make love to me now."

"Are you crazy?"

"For perfectly selfish reasons this is what I want right now."

"Did I interrupt something by coming home?"

"You could lick, dear. You could suck. You could kiss me all over. You could play. You can explore. You could use your hands and eyelashes and huff and puff. You could later on stick it in. You could try something you haven't tried before. You could crawl all behind me. You could pretend I am someone else. I *am* someone else. You could pretend I'm a teenage virgin like you see all day. A black woman. A boy. You could push me wherever you want me. You could be surprised. You could surprise me. You could . . ."

She was still talking when he left. She did not seem to notice his going. He believed he should be worried about their child. He was driving off. He thought of going back to do none of the things she was suggesting, but to ask her not to play games, to stand there but not to beat her, to let her rip at him and then to beat her if he had to; but perhaps that was what she had in mind; he kept on driving.

14

HAVING CHECKED out, she felt free to be less unkind; this did not necessarily mean kind. She let him know she really had found a man. She liked it. She didn't say "him." She liked *it*. She didn't mean this had anything to do with sex. She liked the situation. She liked the new developments.

He would try to understand. She was talking like a building contractor.

She was not yet very "emotionally involved."

He did not enjoy this conversation. He was not her colleague.

"Why don't you do the same thing?" she inquired.

"It couldn't be the same," he said.

"I know what you mean. Yes. You don't want to. But you see: *I do.*" For this project she was being cool, rational, decided, and not unkind. There was a little line of fret between her eyes. She realized he might not enjoy the conversation. It was a tentative shadow of a line. He could make it disappear if he avoided making difficulties. "For purely selfish reasons," she said, "this is what I want right now."

She was therefore willing to recall the past since he insisted on reminding her. How they had loved each other. Okay, stipulate that. How he had not taken to another woman despite his discontentment with the years when she was having their baby, then thinking about checking out. Okay, stipulate that, also. "You don't deserve any credit. I don't think it's very important. It says something about your shyness maybe. Or at the most about your, oh, moral code, that's all." She considered the matter fully. "Or maybe you're sort of attached to me."

It seemed odd that this time had really come. This straightforward woman tried to be honest all the way. And worse, she mostly succeeded. He should accept the terms offered. He volunteered that they had to get moving, get on with their fate.

She agreed totally. She was right with him there. She smiled. Yes. Pretty soon she might get to be emotionally involved. He winced at the words. Emotionally Involved sounded like a disease. "It's rotten," he said. She was still smiling. Her eyelids were pink, not red. He was nauseated and faint. The anger down there in his belly could not be let up or it would strike him again in the eye. He had to keep the compartments tight. This was diminishing him, destroying him. Emission control was using up his equipment.

"It's just a not-you," she said. "I'm not emotionally involved with him yet."

"It's indecent," he said.

She shrugged. "I suppose so," she said. "That's your problem."

Deathgrief. No sleep, the seconds floating by like motes on a sun-scarred eye; helplessly he wished to switch himself out of life.

She said, "I don't see why you're jealous. Wanting another man is about twenty-five percent of what I want now. What about the other seventy-five percent? But you're jealous of the smallest fraction, I can see that."

He waited. What did she have in mind? Why is she conducting this education? And what a helpful and discreet wife. She avoided the word *man* as much as she could.

She was thinking. She was looking at him and puzzling and trying to make herself clear. "Okay, here," she said. "Let me show you what I mean." She reached for him. She had never grabbed him that way. "Come on now, stick it in," she said. She patted it. He said nothing. In an athletic maneuver she kept her hand on him and managed to squat on the floor. Then she lay there like a squaw, lifting her skirt so he could see another wink of her. "Go ahead, go on, go on," she said.

He groaned. He wished to refuse this invitation. "I'll just be selfish," he said.

"I know." She averted her eyes as he tried. She helped with her fingers. Okay. Okay. Okay.

"I'd like to stay here with you now," he said a few moments later.

"Okay." But she removed herself. She bustled about, doing dishes, nails, hair, applying some sort of cream that smelled like Vicks—"I've had this rash," she said. "Emotion, I suppose."

He slept with her in their bed. He awoke after an hour, the sheet twisted, said aloud, not about the sheet, It's sad; reached for her, she moved away, he reached again; in her sleep she held his hand and stroked to stroke him back to sleep. She wanted not to be bothered. He straightened the sheet. She took his hand again. They got up together and he drove the child to nursery school.

He felt like a divorced father now. A really bad fuck should help in some cases. Was that what he meant? No. An uncomfortable night. A twisted sheet. A distracted wife, a sad distracted wife, too.

The next day she called him at school. "You monster," she said. "You creep. You lower than the lowest. You selfish, you stupid, you have no conception of yourself, you dumb, you ugly —"

"What?" he pleaded. "What have I done? What's the matter?"

"I was just thinking of what you did last night," she said, suddenly calmed, and hung up.

He went to look at his face in the mirror. She must be right about him, because it was foolish and monstrous to want sweetness from a woman who wanted to give him nothing, and thus he was a creep, monster, lower than the lowest, selfish, stupid, stupid, stupid—

That was all he had to work with at the moment.

A boy who didn't seem to know he was the Assistant Principal was staring at him as if about to ask for his hall pass.

The weather between them was changeable; this was what was real. It was her birthday—this was *really* real. The little Italian place where they usually celebrated her birthday, just the two of them, would hold the old table for them. Angelo remembered them. The same cake. The same single candle. The bottle of Chianti. The pasta, the veal, the flan. The reality.

As they ate, Angelo hovered. He may have wondered why they talked so little to each other. They emitted wan smiles at each other. Angelo asked if they had been ill, they said no, and so Angelo said they looked very well. They did not quarrel with his logic.

They felt a grace and respite of a sort on this evening. In the parking lot he heard the cinders spitting under the wheels of his automobile like rain mysteriously coming from below. Without saying a word or asking her, he took her to the little furnished apartment which he had just rented by the week.

"I'd like to see it," she said, and then: "Not bad, it's not so bad." He shrugged. "I'm worried about you," she said. "It's really depressing. You should bring your laundry home."

She rushed about, snatching up socks, towels, shirts, and said, "You get no sympathy from me for these things, but I want you to be a neat person, you know. I'll just throw these things in the machine at home."

The way she said *home* included both of them. It seemed that way to him.

On the Goodwill couch she leaned into his arms and said she thanked him for dinner, for her birthday presents (a blouse, a book, a record, a collection of cautious tokens), and she also thanked him for . . . She did not finish the sentence. She rested in his arms.

Slowly and timidly he began to caress her. She did not stiffen. She closed her eyes. She used to complain that, with him, caresses always led to sex. Now he caressed her as he would stroke a cat. Caressing a cat did not lead to sex. She was his cat. He loved his cat. He too closed his eyes. He did not allow himself to be aroused when his fingers lightly trembled over her breasts. This time not. He could feel the nipples stir beneath silk. He did not change the rhythm. Cat.

"Tomorrow," he said, "would you like to have dinner, maybe a movie tomorrow?"

She did not answer. It was as if she were dozing, coiling in her sleep.

"I'll even call the baby-sitter for you," he said.

She did not answer.

"There's a Hungarian place—"

Abruptly she sat up, his arms were no longer around her, she stood up, she was exploding with rage: "Where's my elbow room? You just want to go barreling back together, you just want to move right in together! You don't hear a thing I say! You don't notice a thing I do! You think of nothing but what you want!"

He stood up and said very calmly, "It was a nice evening was all."

"Why don't you find yourself a girl? Why don't you fall in love or anything? Why don't you take me home or call a cab?"

He turned his back to her and said, "I'll drive you. Just wait a moment." He went to the bathroom. He ran cold water on his face. He tried to pee but couldn't. He sat on the edge of the tub a moment.

When he returned, she had her coat on. She had put his laundry in a paper grocery sack. The place was neatened. Chairs stood fitted neatly in the scars of the carpet, where they were supposed to stand. The newspapers were piled in a corner near the door.

They walked to his Pinto. "This is an unsafe car," she said. "You should get another. You picked the wrong used car."

He said nothing.

"Thank you for the presents," she said. "It was a nice dinner. Angelo is really sweet, isn't he? It was a nice evening."

He said nothing. He thought about rear-end collisions. He thought about explosions of gas tanks. He thought about dumbness. He thought about the person by his side.

"But why," she said, "after all, why don't you understand?"

He understood. He was only slow. He drove very carefully.

"Thank you for the birthday," she said. "I know it's hard for you. Try to see it's hard for me. Try to understand."

He wished to help her and help himself. He took her to the door and kissed her goodnight, a teenage date, like their first teenage date, but then said, "I'd like to look at the kid, okay? I'll take the baby-sitter home."

"She just lives next door." She hesitated. "Of course, come in and look at our kid."

He walked straight through to the child's room. It was a stranger's house, but he knew the way. He stood by the bed. He wanted to stay longer, but his wife was walking back and forth, had paid the baby-sitter, was fretful, was worried, was afraid he would make a scene, was thinking what to do, was growing angry.

"Night now," he said.

It felt late, but it was barely midnight. The streets of the city were muffled. He felt a crackling in his ears. He kept busy swallowing and swallowing.

Part / II

1

KNOCK KNOCK. The knock of demand, the knock of discipline, the knock of anxiety, the knock of duty, the knock of bureaucracy, the knock of responsibility, the knock of exasperation. The knock of someone needing him to do something. The knock of interruption. They didn't just pull open the door when it was shut. They knocked. What made them think this was what he preferred?

Just now he preferred them to go away. "Come in," he said.

He had been sitting in his office with his head in his hands, his eyes soothed in the warm palms, feeling lucky for having a job. A nervous breakdown is easier to handle when a fellow needs to take eight hours out of it each day to do his job. Weekends are bad, but from eight to four—his shift at the Assistant Principal's office—he pays attention to the buttons on the telephone, the pencils, the pads, the memos, the paperclips for twisting, the interruptions from ghostly scared young women and daringly mustachioed young men who only plan to teach a few years until they "get my act together."

That hard knock at the door, at his aching eye. The knock of I need help. The knock of a teacher dragging a kid along.

He blinked twice to get both eyes working in tandem. "I said come in! Enter!"

Ted Hansell, little guardsman's moustache, short layered slabs of hair, a fit body with the brown teeshirt showing over the unbuttoned top button of his yellow washnwear shirt, had a black kid by the elbow, holding it high as if demonstrating an elbow specimen, and he was raging. "This boy spit in the fountain. He spit on the floor. He spits at the other students. I tried to handle it myself, but I saw that look in his eye—"

"You saw what look?"

"He was getting fixed to spit at me! If his parents can't deal with him, I think this kid goes to Special School, I think this kid —"

"Okay, okay, okay, Ted, I presume you brought him here in the thought I can handle it. Mr. Hansell, why don't you return to your class and I'll have a chat with—"

"His name's Lester."

"With Lester. How old are you, Lester?"

"He's eleven."

"I asked Lester. How old are you, Lester?"

There was a brief silence. "Man told you."

He said to Ted Hansell: "I'll talk with you later. Thank you for thinking of me. You can go now."

It seemed like a flounce in Ted's departure. There's no good way for a man to display anger through buttocks action. Lester stood there with his lips pouting and his cheeks full. Then the boy swallowed and that was a relief.

"Why don't we talk about what's going on here?" he asked.

He leaned his long sinus headache in the direction of the boy. "Why do you spit so much?"

"I don't spit so much."

"Why do you spit too much, anyway?"

The kid shook his head, meaning *I dunno* or *I ain't telling.* He waited a while. No more answer coming just now.

"Your parents work?" he asked.

"Mom unemploy. Don't know about my dad."

"Oh. I'm self-unemployed," he said. "Does that seem funny to you?" And while the kid was still shaking his head *no,* he asked: "You see your dad?"

"Met him once," the boy said.

"Don't spit," he warned, "no one likes a spitter. Maybe you don't care about being liked. But nobody enjoys a spitter, either. Does that make a difference to you?"

The kid shook his head. He couldn't tell if this meant it made a difference or it didn't.

"Suppose I spit with you. Suppose we have a spitting contest, who can spit further. We got to think of something, kid, or we spit you out of here and send you to Special School. You wouldn't like that, you know?"

"I rather spit with you, man."

The boy looked at him balefully through small red Idi Amin eyes. He was looking through the assistant principal and seeing trouble. The assistant principal had asked the boy about his parents and the boy had not been able to say. Well, if the boy had asked about his wife, he wouldn't have been able to say, either. He would prefer a spitting contest with a sullen black kid with shrewd caution in his voice and a cheekful of weaponry. Interclassroom ballistic saliva. A menace to anyone's peace of mind, seat, and eye.

The kid made his way to school through streets where the burnt-out junkies waited in the doorways, watched from their

Fords by overweight cops who only interfered if they trespassed on the school yard, or if they sold more than a handful, or if the mayor was in the neighborhood. The kid saw his father once, and if his father was one who sold in ten-dollar portions, if he was burnt-out, the kid would not be surprised, he could keep his own saliva flowing. He looked at the kid and thought: Me too, I might prefer to be burnt out, with No Trespassing signs printed all over me. He said: "You know what a school psychologist is?"

"I seen one a those."

"He help you any?"

"She."

"She do anything for you?"

The boy reached into his pocket and took out a stained piece of paper, unfolded it, and deposited a gob into it. Then he carefully replaced the paper in his pocket. There was no force in the gesture. The assistant principal wondered if this was a progress or merely a weakening. He said: "I had some troubles recently. My family. My wife. I talked with someone on that occasion."

The boy took the paper back out of his pocket and looked at it. But this time he didn't unfold it.

"It helped to talk. I was mad. I felt like yelling and screaming, and I did."

The boy grinned. "Bet you didn't spit."

He smiled, too, a co-conspirator. "It might have been a good idea."

"Ain't no idea, a goober," the boy said.

"You know about the cowboys? They used . . ." He decided it was a poor idea to speak of guns. He hummed softly to himself as the boy scratched a small pink ear. "Lassos." The boy looked puzzled. "Ropes."

"You gonna tell my mom?"

"She's been called before, I imagine."

"Sometime she not home when they call."

"I'd rather not do that if you and I can come to an agreement about this spitting matter, Lester."

"Nobody else home you can talk to."

"About this little spitting deal, Lester."

The kid was waiting. The kid had a look in his eye which he would like to call, if he had someone indulgent to talk with when the day was over . . . he would like to call the kid's look *expectorant.* His new life was good training in keeping his bad jokes to himself. Something he had mentioned earlier must come to pass soon or it was just idle jabber, which this situation couldn't afford. "How about we stand at the window here behind my desk"—the kid followed him—"and we see who can make it furthest out there into that courtyard? There's no wind. You can go first."

The kid wasn't sure about this crazy principal. He might have wanted to laugh, but at the proposal of a contest, for the first time he looked scared. Not his mother, not the school psychologist, not transfer to Special School seemed to scare him. But this idea and person with the grownup troubles he didn't know about: this scared him. The boy's face looked purplish, the equivalent of pale, under the darkest opaque African black. This big old white assistant principal grinning like a thing on teevee and suddenly hunkering down on the floor near him, smelling like soap and sweat, trying to collect spit like a real person, wanting to try some fooling around with him, this thing scared him. The assistant principal was mumbling, "Standing Indoor Olympic Spitting Contest: Hey, Lester, you ready?"

"Wha wha what you say?"

"I'm sorry. There's a little wind. Careful spitting against the wind, Lester."

Only wind around here this big white man make.

"There are laws against what we're doing, Lester, it's like pissing and shitting on the street or on people's floors, but if it's just us two here alone and make it kind of nothing but a *game*—"

"I'm not a ball you can bounce," Lester said.

Philosopher, the assistant principal thought.

"You playing with me," the kid said.

"Philosopher," he said, to the boy's evident puzzlement. "The way you stop a ball from bouncing is you put a hole in it to let the air out. Is that what you think I do?"

The kid shrugged. He had made his statement. He didn't understand this stuff. The tidy, springy little kid was wound up tight with care. The coils were tense. No wonder he needed to let go with a gob now and then.

The contest was with an eleven-year-old black kid with slightly parted lips. The boy's tongue looked smaller than his. Well, he was only eleven. It looked gray. There was nothing frightening about it. Lester was eleven and sad. He was thirty-six and sad. "Stop trembling," he said to the boy. "I'm just older. I'm just bigger. I'm just the assistant principal. Your whole life lies ahead of you."

"What you tellin me?"

"Why do you do what you do, son?"

I ain't your son. "I got to fill up time here, nothin else but school here."

"Spitting won't fill up the time, lad." (I ain't your lad.) "Lots of people have tried that. Time is endless." (I ain't rational, mister.)

"I spose."

"I'm not asking for an apology. I assume you're sorry already, if only because you have to come in here and listen to me. Maybe I'm not making a lot of sense. Maybe you won't understand. But for reasons of my own, I don't want to punish you.

I want you to try seeing what it feels like on the other end of spitting. You're there when it lands, son." (Did it again.) "You don't like it a bit, and you don't respect the person who does it, you don't fear it, you're just mad . . ." He paused. "You're just pissed is all. I want to get this true to you, get this *through* to you, boy." (Now I understand this geek. He calls me boy.)

"Everybody's got worries in his life. I got some bad ones. Why don't you tell me what's worrying you?"

Silence. Footsteps and yelling in halls.

"I suppose I should tell you mine, that would be fair, I got some bad family troubles, there's more to it than that. What about you?"

Silence.

"My wife and I . . ."

Silence. Silence from both of them. Double-faced silence.

The assistant principal sighed. "Some people fight to keep warm. They tear themselves apart to keep warm. Do you spit to keep warm?"

"Get *them* hot," the boy said.

"You felt angry, I suppose—mad. So you spit it out?"

"Don't spose," the boy said. "You teachin me, teacher. Got to go *on* somebody."

He looked at the boy with a choking rage in his chest. "That's not the end of the line for either one of us. That doesn't clear it up, Lester. You look at me now." The boy was looking at him. He was in danger. Better think of some good answer right away. Lester the Spitter was waiting. Lester was not ready to be his good buddy. Lester's troubles were not the same as his. Lester was forming his disdain and rage in his smooth young cheeks.

"Okay," said the assistant principal, "let's see who can make it furthest out this window. You first."

The little sudden wet simmer in the dust of the yard was something to aim for, reach beyond.

2

HE LIKED to tell her about the spitter. He needed something outside himself to talk about. Lester was not really a case outside; it was his own case, his client, as the itinerant school psychologist would say, the one who went from school to school, spending most of his time driving and parking. He thought Lester might interest his wife. She could see he was still concerned about his work. He wasn't just interested in her. And he could still interest her in what interested him. And if he could, that was good.

"Hi," he remarked to his wife, "funny thing happened at school today—"

She stood above him on the stairs and said, "I'm really kind of busy, I'm going crazy, if you could take the kid out? Could you?"

"Okay."

"I'm sorry. I'd really like to talk, but you know how I am about *details*. It's been one of those days."

"I understand," he said.

"Sweet, that's sweet of you," she said.

"There are no mere details, I'm a little like that myself," he said.

He tried to think: ice cream, park, zoo, catch with a ball, visit a friend (who?), drive and hope for something to happen, tell her there are adventures in the world as a person grows up . . . The child was already dressed and waiting for him. Another mere detail! She didn't want to go out. She had come up with an idea. Just like an adult, she had awakened from a nap unhappy with the world. She said: "Poopoopants Daddy, you don't even live here anymore."

"Oh, come on, don't say that," his wife said. "I've got some chores, I'm leaving—"

"Poopoopants doesn't." A defiant bland blue stare was emitted from the dear head like a special program—*This is a test of the emergency broadcast system.*

He could handle the spitter. He could handle himself with the spitter. He thought he could handle Lester and himself, but he wasn't sure. This was something he didn't need to test himself against, this anger and spite from his daughter.

Surely he would learn to deal with this detail, too.

"I think I'd like to take the kid for a weekend," he said.

His wife turned on him her most hilarious, loving, large-toothed smile. "Oh, would you? Oh, that would be so sweet. I knew you'd think of it eventually, dear."

"How about this weekend?"

"Right, right, right." She was prepared with the arrangements immediately. "I'll get her things ready. Look, you come here Saturday morning and have breakfast with us—*don't* call Daddy that, darling—we'll have eggs and muffins, bran or raisin, which do you prefer? I'll have all sorts of jams and honeys, and you can take some to your place, a care package, dear, and—"

"You remember what I like."

"Of course I do. You like good things *and* junk."

She was very busy. If she had a lover, he seemed to feed her a lot of coffee.

She knew she was moving too fast. She stopped and looked into his face with a calm gratitude. "I really appreciate your offering," she said quietly. "That's nice."

"Offering what?"

He saw little flecks on his daughter's lips, like melting snowflakes, the active spurting glands of a child; and in his own mouth, hot corrosive saliva burned; all the world can spit, he decided.

She thought better of her tenderness. It always led to difficulties. "Oh, that's wonderful," she was saying. "Honey, you're going to spend the weekend at your nice daddy's nice new place!" And she turned back to him: "What was it happened at school? Something interesting, dear?"

3

ON SATURDAY he awakened before his clock radio did its top forty job on him. A relief. He tried to unravel out of his dreams without that startle of rock or deejay good cheer.

He came blinking from the maze, and as usual, forgot his sleeplife immediately. In due course he might deal with it. He stretched and sighed. A weekend with his daughter. They would explore the domains of single parenthood, wouldn't they? Together at last—one kid, one dad. He worked his face in the grayness of the room, and found a glint of early sunlight on the silent radiator, and made of these facts—that he was not paralyzed, that there was sun, that the radiator was silent—a set of good auguries. He would cherish his child. She wouldn't say Poopants, no it was Poopoopants Daddy. He would have that nice muffin breakfast with her and with his wife emeritus.

He could jump up and into a cold shower. He was a healthy

fellow, no heart attack from icy showers. He liked the idea of waking up that way rather than with coffee. No poopoopants daddy this one.

But he decided to wait for his shower today; a jolt of coffee first. He pulled the shade all the way up, he parted the curtains wide, he opened the window. He wanted his furnished "executive suite" to look friendly to his child, and sunny, and clean, and not at all poopoopants. He was going to be happy. There was only one person to please, his daughter. He did not have to please a wife. He had only two people to please, his child and himself.

Slowly getting things straight, he thought. He whistled. He projected joy to the world. He climbed into his used Volvo— had retired the Pinto—and it started. Starts in the Swedish winter, starts here; therefore everything really okay. He switched on the classical station. Everything works when you get things straight, he thought. It's just the two of us now.

He was whistling along with a morning dose of baroque music and practicing hard to feel good, getting ready for breakfast muffins with his nearly former wife and his present child. He was blowing the blood into the capillaries of his cheeks. He would have slept all night in the out of doors of this city, if such had been possible without looking shipwrecked, like a veteran panhandler, in the morning.

The house was quiet, Saturday quiet. He expected it to be swelling and throbbing with family life, radios, appliances, attachments, the bodies fitting themselves into one body, as in their foolish contented marriage. He rang. He would carry the child's bag and toys down after breakfast. His wife would offer him a few muffins in a bag for tomorrow morning. Rang again. No one answered. Sleep? Still asleep? Someone answered.

This was different. The door opened, and his wife stood in a nightgown hastily thrown over her body, bow at the neck not tied (this neat wife tied her bows when she went to bed), and she looked sleepy, bemused, embarrassed, happy, a summer-breeze play of feeling across her face; the soft girlish puffiness of pleasure and sleep and pink and more pleasure.

"You're not awake yet!" he said, astonished.

Still smiling sleepily, she said, "You can't come up."

"What?" A thickness in his head kept the wheels turning as they had been set: pick up child, breakfast together, the three of them, chatter, good-by, a kiss good-by to mommy, muffins to go, good-by.

"You can't come in."

"You said?"

She was just smiling that peaceful, calm, sleepy, slightly embarrassed, pleased little smile and the undone pink ribbon bow on her new nightgown moved festively as she shook her head.

"I said you can't come in."

"What?" He didn't understand, or didn't want to.

"Something came up. Can't come in. I'm sorry about breakfast, that's all it is." But she wasn't sorry; she was smiling. Yes, she was sorry; the twitch was embarrassment. No, she wasn't sorry, yes she was, no she—

Poopoopants daddy, he thought.

He didn't move himself forward into the hallway. It was a momentum from elsewhere that moved him forward. Surely it was not his doing. It was the spirit that put the spit in Lester's cheeks. It was behind him, pushing; in his bone, exploding. As he moved, so did she, till they were touching. The undone bow. His chest. She was barring the door. "You can't come in," she said again. He thought he had stopped. With his mind he stopped. But like a laser light into his eyes, into some primitive root of brain, her sleepy pleased smile set off that momentum of rage and idiocy and he started to push by her toward their daughter upstairs; he pushed—he pushed her breast behind the warm pink bow. The breast was soft and warm; his finger brushed a nipple.

"Couldn't you wait till I'm gone? What was that about breakfast and a muffin? Couldn't you wait till—couldn't you ask him to wait an hour?"

"This was last night. I wasn't thinking so far ahead."

He wanted upstairs. He wanted his child. He wanted to see the breakfast table. He pushed at her shoulder to get by and heard the sound of his open hand on her flesh.

"Don't!" she cried. *"Hal!"*

There was a heavy stir, a rushing trample, and a man stood at the top of the stairs. The child, still in her sleepybear nightgown, stood behind the man. The man, naked, his arm on the railing, was ready to fling himself down the stairs to protect the woman who had called out his name, appealed for his protection —*Hal*! The assistant principal, dressed in Saturday jeans, unstrung by getting up early, looked up at the naked man at the head of the stairs, his daughter behind the man, and felt uncovered. He must have looked at his wife in a peculiar way. Why, that was his own hand on her, pushing her to reach for the child behind the jungle tangle of sex, hair and pink, a dark coil of snake in a curly tangle, his daughter hiding behind the man.

"Hal!"

But if his wife was terrified, why was she still smiling that peaceful, pleased, alert smile?

The man moved a step down the stairway, his thick dark shaft bobbing and shifting. He folded his arms on his chest. "Hey, what the fuck you doing in here?" Hal inquired.

His wife was still smiling, or so it seemed.

Well, he could buy his own muffins and toast them.

"Send the child down, I'll wait outside," he said.

Driving and driving, he was thinking, There's my daughter here, mustn't kill or die.

He carried her plastic bag with toys, books, clothes for the weekend into the gritty smell of the front hall of his new flat. The child turned her face to his and said sweetly, distractedly, with her cheekbone catching the light where her tears touched it, "Poor poopoopants, we don't even live there anymore, do we, Daddy?"

4

He drove an automobile he would never use to kill himself.

In a drawer he kept a folding knife he would never use.

His heart was fisting open and shut, unwilling to let him stop his life.

He had a child with him, but when he looked in the rearview mirror, he saw the hair and meat of a man made gloomy by being taken from his rest and pleasure—Hal's body pasted on the mirror. On his retina Hal floated as he blinked and blinked to try to blink him away.

I'm the buddha known as The Fuckup. (Choose words more carefully.) I'm the buddha known as the fucked up. This here assistant principal, sometimes acting principal, with a knack for dealing with the spitting problem among eleven-year-olds, who only wants to be cuddled, is a secret mayhem man. *Have You*

Remembered to Smash & Kill? Do You Always Mess Your Life Like That?

Hal was off his rearview mirror and retina now; Hal was in his stomach.

"Daddy! Car!"

"Darling, you're right, I'll slow down."

The child watched his face without interrupting his thoughts. The child knew he was busy. The daddy patted her knee and said, "You're right. It's okay. Don't be afraid."

"Daddy," she said. Don't *you* be.

The city, wires, pipes, billboards, stores, streaks of automobiles, streaks of drying tears, a tunnel around them. He burrowed through this tunnel.

I change my oil when the warranty book says I should. I do my job and pay my dues and plan to collect my pension. I think about my school. I stop the spitting when I can. I'm an assistant principal who doesn't lick asses of superintendents and principals and other assistant principals, not more than absolutely necessary. I loved a woman. Why am I not getting what I want? She doesn't love me, doesn't love me, doesn't, I can't let go.

Christopher Columbus left his pains and comforts behind in order to give birth to himself in a new world. He did what he intended to do, and came back in chains. But what was my discovery, my new world? She was. What was my loss and bondage? She is. I merely lost a woman. No America, no world, no destruction or horror—just everything rolled up into one unexplored continent of woman. I don't have her anymore; no history; the past denies itself. I'm a humorist who supplies no laughs.

When he remembered her in a hurry, when he had only a moment to remember her in, because a door was opening, a teacher was calling, a meeting was beginning, he would remember sliding into her body, the sexual fact leaping up like a hungry and ragged flame, that warm clutch and gasp of doing it. But when he floated in memory, he thought of looking at her across the table at Sunday breakfast—she buttered the toasts, she sampled his egg ("in case it's poisoned," she said, licking the fork); or running down to the beach on a hot day and she turned and grinned at a kid's sand tower that looked like a phallus ("I'll be right back!"); or touching at her hip, his hip, bumping when they walked; or the silence in a long automobile ride—what was it, pride? what was it, lust? what was it, merely settling down? He loved her. He had loved her. Once when they quarreled, just before they married, he said, "But think of the children!" and she said, "We don't have any yet," and he said: "That's the point." She laughed and they sealed their reconciliation in the usual way. Now he tried unsuccessfully to remember why they had quarreled; it must have been just fraying together too much.

A thing is what it is, he thought, and thus it is not another thing. So why make this wifiness or possessingness or need of mine or need of her or claim on us something else? It's not the meaning of life. It shouldn't, he thought, it shouldn't even be the cause of all my joy. Was it? Do I remember correctly? Once she clamped her legs like a slim quarterback's around his neck; he was linked by them with the world. She squeezed some of his life out; she injected him with the need of her. Sometimes he even winced when she invited him to climb on with her, when she said, "It's a nice night. Look at that moon. I feel sexy. Let's go."

He had to care about her heat and gestures, not her words, because her words made him sad and her gestures made him happy. Did, did, did. He wasn't sure anymore they did. Times have changed. Mother mine, he thought.

I'll bet being an assistant principal in a junior high school could lead to a career in education, he thought. I need a career change. I need something that gives me a way out, maybe a job at Burger King University, teaching the nineteen-year-old Management Trainees to be twenty-year-old Managers. I could talk charcoal broiling, time clocks, and hair in the cole slaw. I could get out of town, that's what I could do.

Oh, I'm changing, I'm changing from spouse that was, I can tell, it makes me sad not to be myself, I'm not the man who was loved by her, I'm someone else and don't know who. Tell me, tell me, tell me: Who am I without her?

Did you remember to answer the question?

I miss her, he thought, remembering the hollows of her body where he liked to fall asleep, his cheek pressed against the warmth of veiny faraway places. He didn't know whether or not to be ashamed of the memory.

Best to be neither ashamed nor unashamed but to forget.

His daughter sat there as he drove. When she had cried at the sight of his flat, and she had not really known why, since it was fun to play house, and she didn't say anything more than she could say, this child who called him poopoopants because she was sad and worried, the tears had marked her cheekbone with light and he saw the lean strong face to come, the face that would emerge out of babyflesh and time, the face of his wife. But now she was watching his lips move; she was pale and comprehending, like a deaf child learning new skills. "I like your stories, dad. Hal doesn't talk to me, even when he throws me up and up and catches me and makes me laugh too much."

"Is that like tickling?" he asked.

"It's fun though," she said.

5

IN THE second floor hall, East, he heard the pretty substitute Spanish teacher say to another teacher: "Let's go out and diet together tonight."

He tucked that away. Melanie Volk. Maybe he would have to get better acquainted with her. Melanie, Melanie, such a pretty name. Volk, Volk, means wolf, doesn't it? Maybe first he should get interested in her and not merely pretend to himself. Let's go out and get interested in something together tonight, Melinda, no, Melanie. Let's think about it. Let's try maybe next week. I'll brush up my Spanish charm.

Then he had just swung back in his chair when the phone rang and a lightly accented voice said, "It is your friend."

"Who?"

"Your friend from near Oslo back near you."

"Oh, hello . . ." And the rest unrolled very rapidly. He

couldn't remember her face, her name, her body, her voice; he was occupied; he was distracted; he was so happy to hear from her; no, he couldn't see her just now, it was a bad week, the whole week was a bad week, so sorry. FOOL BASTARD *I just lost all compassion for HE*

He was tending to business even if it was bankrupt business.

Should he take a leave of absence from his job? Nervous break-around; is that a disease? Was he doing anything for the school? What about the Spitter, had he checked on Lester? Was he looking after things and tidying up?

Not well enough. But if he stepped away from his job, got a medical excuse, he could get it, Board approval was likely, *then* he would break down. That was the problem. The job was holding him together when the rest of his life stopped doing assigned tasks.

He had come to this career because he liked kids and keeping busy and it was too late in his endocrine system for him to be a mother. He could be a father, but that wasn't the same thing. He thought of himself as a nurturing person; also needed to be nurtured. He thought he wanted a strong wife; he got one, strong for herself. For what person was he strong? Who would be strong for him now?

Poor Lester. Someone should take an interest. He strolled down the hall, a healthy school bureaucrat, smiling, preoccupied, an unwhistled whistle pursing his mouth, to pick up the kid at studyhall time before lunch.

"Lester," he said. "I'm the assistant principal."

"I know what you are."

"How are you doing?"

"I suppose so."

"That isn't what I asked. Want to go out for an ice cream cone?"

"That ain't what you axe me for, neither."

"I'm asking."

The kid grinned. He ran toward him. "Yeah, do," he said. His hair smelled of burning paper. He must have stood near a trash fire.

"I tell you what, let's get in the car."

The kid didn't know and didn't care. He took Lester to a cafeteria in a bowling alley, WEST SIDE BOWLING, and they ate jello together, cafeteria food, fruit jello, sitting up straight and looking carefully away from each other, talking with the strained manners of a father and son who don't know each other very well. The thump of bowling balls, and the cavernous tumble of pins. The Hall of the Mountain Kings, he thought. It's better than eating alone.

"I like this stuff, this canned-fruit jello," said Lester.

Much better, he thought. I spent nice times eating with her, but also boring times. Even the boring times were boring times with my wife. I expected they would be less boring later. I waited too long. "More?" he said to Lester. "More fruit jello?"

"Prefer," said the kid, "a hotdog now. I'm hungry. This stuff not for when you hungry."

He watched the kid eat fruit jello, then a hot dog, then another, then ice cream, then hot chocolate, and said: "Now maybe you'd like to meet my daughter."

"How old she?"

"Too young for you, just a baby. You can meet my wife, too."

The spitter was surprised by nothing. He shrugged and sucked his tooth. Probably needed dental care he wasn't getting. He looked out the window at streets he didn't know. He didn't care. He would go anyplace with this funny principal man; made no never mind.

"Hul-lo," said his wife, "who's this?" She bent with her radiant and entertained smile to greet the boy. "How are you?"

"Lester. I like this kid. He's not been absolutely ruined yet," he said.

"Lester," said the kid. "Guess I ain't been ruined, do I?"

"Well. You're making new friends," she said to her husband.

"He ought to go to the dentist. It's on my way. Tell her, Lester. I think everyone needs a friend, even us two."

Lester grinned. "I never did."

"You're the humblest boy that ever praised himself. *You do, Lester.*"

The boy touched his hand. His mom couldn't find a dentist. The man knew how. He was in the habit of fighting and spitting. Maybe he'd stop awhile. He had plenty of time to take the matter under advisement.

"I thought I'd take her with us," he said, "get her out of your hair awhile. I can sit with her—"

"She'll be bored."

"I'll be reading to her. She'll be in my lap if she wants to. I'll take responsibility for her boredom."

Lester was chewing his gum and sucking his tooth. The boy was watching the wife. He had a dark, shiny, cautious look in his eyes. He knew about babies and if this dude wanted to bring one along, that was okay. She looked at Lester and her husband as if they were a team, but not one she wished to oppose.

"Okay," she said, "you want to keep her overnight? That happens to be convenient, too."

His belly turned. "Okay," he said.

To the dentist he praised his kindness for taking them on such short notice. Lester didn't even show fear. He and the child would wait here for Lester, and if his mother said okay, Lester too could spend the night at the assistant principal's. Lester saw nothing unusual in this. He often spent the night in different places.

His own child. He sat in the waiting room drawing pictures with his daughter. "You draw me," he said, "and I'll draw you."

"I need a purple one," she said.

"A purple crayon?"

"I need all the colors."

"To draw me?"

"To draw," she said.

"Just use the colors you have," he said, "that's all we can do. Use the ones you have."

She sucked a crayon and tried her best with inadequate equipment.

"I'll try to get you all the colors at home," he said, "but we don't want to go to the store now. We just want to stay here."

"Okay," she said. "If I make a booboo, you won't get mad?"

"I love your booboos," he said. "I make lots of them myself. Are you okay?"

"Okay," she said. "I wish you still lived with us."

He was not so busy with himself that he could not be busy with her. Still, he was very busy with himself.

"Daddy?"

"Were you talking?"

"Were you listening?"

"Don't you like the dentist's crayons?"

On the way home he asked the child: "Do you remember when you called me Poopoopants Daddy?"

"When?"

"A while ago. When you were angry with me?"

"Is that what you were?" she asked.

"That's what you said."

The child shrugged. She turned away. Maybe it was a dumb thing to tell her, a dumb thing to bring it up, poopoopants daddy.

Lester was touching his teeth. "Feel funny," he said.

"That green didn't belong. Doesn't it feel better now?"

"Feel funny," Lester said. "Dirty teeth didn't hurt none, but it just feel funny, don't hurt, neither."

After a dinner of sandwiches, milk—"a lunch, really," he explained to head off any criticism—and apples from which the children each took one polite, disapproving bite, they all brushed their teeth together. It was instructional toothbrushing time. Then he told a story. Lester pretended to be bored. The children lay curled in sleeping bags in opposite corners of his bedroom. They were sleeping in the bedroom. He would sleep on the couch in the non-bedroom. No one would sleep in his bed. It just worked out that way.

After awhile, finishing the newspaper, still not sleepy, still not really awake, he went back to look at the children, his daughter and Lester. If he had remained married, he might have had another. He could not know if his feeling for this fatherless boy, this spitter, was what he might have had for his own son—no, too much, too endless much pity for Lester. He wasn't sure Lester needed that.

Looking at the two children, their damp faces and the childish snores in the halfdark, he thought now he could sleep. He was there and they were here. Everything belonged together. He remembered how it felt to belong with his wife when they curled together in the bed she kept at home as a useful place for all she had to do in it.

Having puttered with the children like a father, he now sought that pleasant feeling after good love with his wife, not the convulsions and cries, but the sleep, the cozy faint, like going under more than going to sleep; that sinking into the reward of sleep with the company of his lady, entangled in their four arms and going under together.

Before they had the child.

Before the child had them.

He made a black grin in the dark at this complaint against all he had for love now, their daughter, who could never divorce him. Bless her. Bless the poor spitter, too.

Still, for peace and a glimpse of heaven, there's nothing like sinking into sleep with love in his arms. It's not sure. It's not trustworthy. It was what he had and what he lost . . . He jabbed himself with a wakeup call: *Your child! your daughter! what matters, thug?*

He blinked. Almost gone. The kids wear out their caretaker. No wonder mothers complain. Stray lights from the street as he hurried to the bedroom, a swimming of drowsiness in the air.

The spitter was sitting up, silently watching the little girl asleep across the room. He was sitting up and the heel of his hand was in his mouth. He had been told not to suck his thumb. He was eating the heel of his hand.

"Lester," he said. "Get down. Sleep."

He shoved and the boy floated down with his eyes shut.

He roamed. He picked up the newspaper which had slid to the floor. In Washington, he noticed, changing the plug for the lamp with the plug for the television, Mr. Kissinger was just returning from a voyage, but about to go elsewhere, before going to a third place. He stared in amazement. Other people were having troubles, too.

Wasn't it odd that Doctor Kissinger looked so contented and sleek with the world's pains, and he, bearing only his personal grief, was looking pure and emaciated with his selfish concentration?

A little figure in the upper corner of the television screen translated Mr. Kissinger's airport insouciance into deaf sign language. This wagging and semaphoring made it seem even more happy a play. The Goodwill teevee set got channels he had never heard of. Perhaps it wanted to bring him in touch with the real world's pains which made Mr. Kissinger thrive so.

He felt like a wornout thug. He lay on the couch fully dressed and closed his eyes. Before he slept, he thought: Try to pay attention to what matters.

Part / III

1

DREAM DHARMA ACADEMY OF EAST-WEST NATIVE AMERICAN HEAL-
ING. Our ongoing holistic vision of eco-human possibility, rooted
in yoga and radical therapies, gives unique succor to interpersonal
lifestyle hangups. Men, call Jehane; Womenpersons, call Jhorge;
Bisexuals, call Seymour. The cosmic rainbow culture of soul &
body anima people awaits you, 24-hour crisis line.

334–4333

THAT'S THE ticket, he thought, studying the Xeroxed message
tacked on the Native Sun Health Foods Superette cork board.
What else have I got to lose? Pride, shame, hangups? Why not?

He bought his wheat germ, his sprouted bran, his copy of
Prevention, his cherry Kefir; he chewed a handful of coconut
granola from the bin; he slipped through his anima. He had a
way to go in eco-human possibility.

Just before his marriage, he had been lifted out of childhood trauma by the psychic judo method. It was the late sixties, but already he had been keenly aware of the future failure of Viet Nam peace to bring peace of soul. The gifts of both prophecy and pessimism, plus a kind of intelligence, had helped find him a job as assistant principal in an inner city junior high school. He wanted stability, a new Toyota, a role in his wife's eyes. And now, after years of personal growth and lack of it, marriage and the failure of marriage, he was seeking a consultation at the bulletin board of the Native Sun (No Cans, No Preservatives, Chickens Without Hormones).

He sank a dime in the pay telephone at the corner. 334-4333.

"Hullo, Jehane here," called a cheery voice, pronouncing as Joanne.

"Uh, Fuh-fred Farr, I'm interested in the interpersonal life-style hangup program."

"Private or group?"

"Private," he said.

"Fuh-far out, Fuh-fred—" Her chuckly relaxation indicated she was used to false names. "Why'nt you truck on over for a private lesson in fighting and loving, how to accomplish an honest interaction with your interpersonal mate? The first lesson is free, plus a twenty-dollar contribution to the Academy. After the first free lesson you can choose to share a contribution to me, depending on the mere details of your karma. Bring a towel, some oil, and the exact date and time of day of your birth. Never mind the oil, Fuh-fred, you wouldn't have the right kind anyway."

He was not sure he wanted to go so far out for cure. He had been so far in with young marriage, young fatherhood, young career, this was terra very incognita. The thought convinced him. He had gone too far in; he needed to go out again. The Dream Dharma Academy and Jehane did not simply appear in Xerox on a cork board by accident. There was a power in the universe. The world is a nest of meaning.

He checked his pockets for keys, wallet, corridor pass. He hated this nervous habit. Living alone was killing him.

After dismissal of school on Monday, he drove to the warehouse and railroad district where the Dream Dharma Academy had its world headquarters. This is not a gypsy, he thought. This is not steal your money, give you a disease. I'll bet this is a young hippie healer who has given up dope and has strong hands.

World Headquarters needed no vulgar self-display or status-seeking. There was a tree of heaven in the yard, a blue VW van parked near it. There were potatoes in soy products cans at the windows, sprouting pale green tendrils. There was a friendly creak of wooden porch as he mounted. KNOCK. CHIMES IN RE-PAIR.

"Hi, I'm—"

"You say you're Fred," said the plump young woman with brilliant shining moles on her cheeks. "That answer, my friend, is blowing in the wind."

"I have to say I'm not sure of you, either," he remarked with dignity (upward mobile junior high assistant principal making a desperation recovery move).

"Faith moves mountains," she said, "and that's why there are no mountains in the midwest. All the mountains have been moved to Colorado and California and Nepal and high-energy places like that. Won't you come in?"

"I'm in. Thank you."

"Won't you *really* come in?"

"Um—will you make yourself clear? I'm depressed, I'm literal."

She went into what started like a wink but finished like a small, take-out trance. "I feel you have horny troubles. Troubles you have. Sadness you have. Sleepless you have. Fatigue and sinus." She opened her eyes. "Grief."

"That's the exact word I use for myself," he said, playing for time.

"Sit down first. Then we make love in a strickly instructional first encounter of the karma. Unless you're some Capricorn with freaky stuff in mind, in which case try Masters and Johnson. You'll have to travel to Illinois for that, So-Called Fred."

"Indiana?"

"One of those towns. Geography's not my strong suit, except for the chart of the heavens. That I got down. You brought your materials? Here. Give."

Her arms were fleshy. The flesh hung like strong protein. It didn't wobble when she spoke nonsense. Later, when all this would be forgotten, it might wobble even when she spoke sense. But he wouldn't care about Jehane when he had forgotten his wife, the only woman he wanted, and the world had forgotten him. The sky outside was as blue and glassy as a fortune-teller's ball. Jehane's eyes were as blue as the sky, a babe's eyes, floating somewhere above the arms of a butcheress.

"Tell me your false name again," she said.

"Fuh-fred."

She grinned, showing her back teeth. She had never been burdened with braces. The teeth were mostly healthy. One was of healthy gold, a thick thump of metal in the mouth. Maybe she was part gypsy after all. She was the modern heir to a gypsy tradition. He felt his wallet. "Take it off," she said, "all of it."

Would she ask to bless his money? Would she say his money was cursed and needed to have the hex removed?

"Your wango has bad karma," she said, "so let's dust the whole thing off and see what we can do for you."

He stood waiting in front of her. He was just following orders. She squinted and did a survey.

"Uh, I'm sort of a married man," he said.

"The more reason to improve all you can. You get to use that little thingie regularly, I hope."

"Separated. She doesn't love me anymore."

"They never do, friend Fred. They never love you fellas enough. Sigh all you want. Okay, sigh. Sigh now, please." He did so. "That's right. That's the sentence of life."

He stood shivering.

"Romance gets you loved afresh. Think of this lay as a probe —a romance, So-Called Fred."

"I'm worried about my marriage. We're living apart—separated. I'm not ready to let go."

"That's good, talk up a blue storm as I lead you through the Eleven Steps for Better Loving. Fact is, howsomever, it's best you turn off your head. Ride with the flow, sing with the song. Let go one thing at a time. Be here and don't be here. Think and not think. You'll finish just fine. I never have one isn't usually just fine by the time I take his money."

"I'm here."

"Notice I don't ask you for the cash until you're finished. Gratitude guarantees I get mine. Okay, So-Called Fred?"

"Okay."

"Magni-far-out-okay?"

In his heart of hearts he had no more okays on hand today. She gazed into his eyes and then made a sound like a cold engine turning over. She felt the air near his body without touching him. She ran her hands down the space two inches from his spine, and then down his chest, up to his jaw, and circled his crotch twice—he could feel the warmth of her hands and her mind although she did not even brush against his pants; she slipped along the airstream interrupted by his legs, socks, shoes; she stood up and stretched. She flexed her fingers. She shook her head. "Your aura," she said. "Your enema." For some reason he remembered his mother. It was that word.

"What?" he asked.

"Your anima," she said. "Tuckered out, brother-person. Come into the sauna with me." She was slipping out of her gypsy granny robe. Within, there was a plump person with purple nipples and a belly dappled with curlicues of fat and a dark, slightly hairy, winking navel. Her not being beautiful reassured him; it seemed sort of sincere. She was not beautiful and she was nice.

He turned his back and let his clothes fall. He picked them up and draped them on a chair. His coins spilled and tinkled and ran, but he was not going to scramble for pennies, nickels, dimes. However, he bent to pick up a couple of quarters.

"Towel," she said. She tossed him a large beach towel which was a little stiff, due to non-fluff drying. She opened the door to the sauna and said Whew while he said Ouch. It was hot. "Feels good," she commanded. "We'll save your towel."

They both concentrated on arranging towels, breathing, saying Ahh, and getting settled. His body submitted; this was a definite plus. Peace of mind began to appear on the distant horizon. The voice of Jehane pealed strong and clear through shimmering heat. "There is a picturesque hinterland, do you know that?"—he nodded on command—"located in the chakra between your asshole and your cock."

He said nothing, playing for time.

"Do you know that?"

"I suppose so."

"No sex in here, this is heart attack territory," she said. "We have to get clean, get organized, talk a little, shower, cool off first. Listen."

He nodded.

"So there's where your metabeing is located. In that hinterland, fella. Your crotch can get the crabs or the premature ejacks, but your chakra is forever."

"Amen," he said.

"Joke if you so wish. It only means you're nervous. I'm not a mumbler of things, since deeds do the trick, not words."

Was he a trick to be done?

She peered at him through the hum of heat. The sweat was popping and drying on his skin. He felt no desire for anyone. He remembered Paul and Paula—well, at least this was fun and that wasn't. He remembered the wife with whom he had had no fun with Paul and Paula. Like his sweat, the past was popping and drying in violent heat. "Listen here, So-Called," Jehane was saying. "Some people get to plan only one day at a time. If they're lucky. They die unplanned. *You* get to think ahead and plan your life as an erotic, feeling, sensate being. So when death comes—" She leaned her dry, hot, pendulous breasts near his nose. He smelled nothing. "When Death comes, you can say with the gods, Hah!"

"Ha," he said.

"Hah!" she cried, correcting him.

"Ha."

"Hah!"

"HAH!"

She scrubbed her thighs with a corner of her towel. "That's better. You're teachable. You're learnable. You'll be okay. You want some fruit juice? Little things people don't know: citrus could possibly be good for your heart. You've got so much to learn, So-Called, about the Phenomenology, what I call, the Phenomenology of Feeling. You ever suspect how much you don't know or feel, So-Called?"

"HAH!"

"Goo-ood," she said, singing the two and a half syllables of that word, "goo-ood, for a start, So-Called. Have you had a tad therapy in your life, mayhap?"

"Some family guidance. Long time ago, some Freudian stuff. In my day, I've looked within."

"Well, I'll say this about that: this isn't that," she reported. "I am *not* a therapist, this is *not* medicine. This here is a *learning* experience. I might advise you, for better orgasm, to double your citrus, cut out your fats, try yeast, but that's the extent. I'm a professional friend and companion is all. There's laws in this state. The AMA is so jealous you wouldn't believe. Want to achieve your shower experience now?"

"Okay."

"Brief terse comments are sometimes right on. I'll let you wash my back. Learn to be my best friend, too."

"That's what I'm paying for," he said.

As they emerged gasping from the sauna, careful not to bump the electric coals glowing in the clean little bin, like a catbox near the door, she issued one of her brief terse communiqués from the non-therapy front: "Joking is one of your avoidance karmas, So-Called. There's an armor of haha around your anima. Inside, you're weeping."

So true. So true.

Shower.

The mysteries and risks of an unfamiliar shower with unpredictable nozzles.

He heaved up a roar from the depth of his being which astonished him and made Jehane giggle while she used the twin stall adjoining. The water shot like arrows against his skin. In the cold he imagined rolling around in the snows of Finland after a sauna. He imagined purity and ice and healthy blood speeding through the veins. He imagined glacial pools after climbing a dusty mountain. He heaved up a howl of heartshock and blood-terror. He didn't even miss his wife.

As he leapt out, Jehane was there, extending a white terry-cloth robe. With the touch of cloth and her hands he was dry; the water flew off his body in little steamlets. Jehane handled him with the carelessness of an expert. She led him to a group of foam cushions on the floor, heaped with a snowdrift of terry-cloth. She pushed him down like a dog. Good dog. She smiled. She arranged him. She stretched his legs and arms and pulled. She pressed. "Shiatsu," she said, "is acupuncture without nee-dles. I'm all thumbs, So-Called. I'm closer to your aura. Your dharma is less so-called than your anima. Shush, baby."

She arranged his lumps. She arranged his soul. She arranged his protuberances. Now he knew what plumbing felt like, if plumbing could feel, in the hands of a compassionate plumber.

—high tension wires in the hands of a master electrician, climbing in the winds of the prairie with spurs and a smile—

—a bolt of white fire—

As he fell, subsided, his mind shot through, a message crossed the terminal. She was the mightiest friend and therapist on earth, on earth, on earth.

"Do you like candy afterwards? Me, I go for fertile eggs right away—something in my other life was a snake, I think—scram-bled?" she asked. "It's included in the honorarium."

He affirmed fertile eggs. He ate soft and nourishing yellows and whites. And the misery flowed back like lava down a moun-tain. It was not supposed to be like this.

"I want my wife," he said, sitting naked, cross-legged, on terrycloth.

"You're a difficult, complex case."

"Maybe I'm just a creature of habit. I'm in love."

She shook her head. She touched a spot on his breastbone. "Your third eye is crossed. So you think you can't live without her."

He said nothing. She let the nonsense fade into the air of sweat, terry, high thermostat.

"I don't know her personally," she said, "but I'd venture a supposition you can't have her. That's a probe. That's a guess."

"She's bored with me, probably good reasons for that," he said, "but I need her."

She observed his grief with the coolness of a consulting specialist. She had training and skills beyond Hippocrates or Mayo. All the benefits of her months of research were brought to practical use by the challenge of a troubled patient.

She asked: "Do you lick soup or do you put the whole spoon in your mouth?"

"I don't know," he said, "depends on how hungry—"

"I'd like to make a best effort with you." She smiled. "Come. It's my job, So-Called." She crooned softly: *As the ship goes out to sea, I push my spoon away from me.*

"What? what do you mean?"

"I'll try everything, So-Called. There is no reason in the world for you not to survive. Fall out of love, please. Your case interests me."

"I'd like to get interested in something else."

"We'll work on it. Follow me."

"I'm doing my best."

"I can never resist the cry from the wilderness. Even if he thinks I'm fat and funny. Even if he thinks I'm foolish. Even someone playing hide-and-go-seek. No matter how he tries to hide the call of pain." Said Jehane, measuring him with smiling eyes of love: "My hangup is helping."

2

SHE DECIDED to explain her new thoughts on the subject. Understanding is an element of progress. Clarity begins at home! He sat, attending carefully.

As an intelligent person ("at least would-be, dear"), she had been puzzled at the persistent nagging sense of error in her life. Disappointment at her ability to make a crucial mistake wasn't even the worst thing about it. She found herself at fault and discovered that not every error could be cleanly remedied. She had been deceived by her own life. She liked herself less for it.

It had taken her a long time to decide (he didn't wince, he gave no sign of life) she didn't love him. Since she had acted as if, felt as if, lived as if, it seemed she must have. Love. But now she didn't. Her own misjudgment had perturbed her deeply. It also, she realized, brought distress into the life of her husband.

How could she not love him and still like this best and closest friend?

A worser puzzle. Just when she had almost tuned out her deep longings enough so that she could accept not loving him, but also accept that she had to make the best of her choice for a while, she began to suspect something new and even more surprising: She didn't like him, either. (Or so she thought.) Why? He hadn't harmed her (he'd married her, though), he hadn't abused her (he demanded that she love him, though), he had intended to make her happy (and gave her a daughter who could not be dismissed from care and plan.) "Thank you for paying attention, dear. I know this is not easy. I hope you understand I blame myself—no, that's not the word—*judge* myself. Sometimes I say it's your problem, but that's unfair of me. It's not just your problem."

He listened. They could agree that regret is like jealousy— does no good.

"When the child's a little older I can do something else. Work. Go to school. In due course I'll figure it out. But I had to do something about this *now*. I couldn't settle for what I didn't want. When I was a girl I was known as the Truth-Teller. Funny thing, some nicknames don't follow you to college, but this one did—"

"I liked that about you."

She waited to make sure he wasn't planning to interrupt. He was still listening despite the fact that he had interrupted. She still liked the truth-telling in herself, which had traveled intact from her girlhood to womanhood, because it partly redeemed so many other things she didn't like; so many errors, boredoms, pains.

Was it fair that she not like her husband simply because they had come to grief? Of course not. Fair is not the issue in such matters. "Try to understand," she said. "You're being very quiet, dear."

She had long days to think about these puzzles. She didn't love the cause of her grief; not loving and feeling grief made her feel bad; so how could she like (never mind love) what continually made her feel bad? "Surely you understand," she said, "an intelligent man like you."

He nodded.

And for a long time she couldn't even explain to her lover and best friend how she didn't love and like him anymore. He would not want to hear it. And by definition he wasn't her lover and best friend, anyway. So it was all tangled and unpleasant, wasn't it?

He nodded.

Oh what sense is there in the long days of tending to a child and waiting for a man to come home, whom you don't want to come home, if you can't at least share the truth with the most important person in your life?

Every time she used to try to explain to him he started to crumble. She wanted a fair listener, not a crumbler.

So she had sat in the park with the other mothers and watched the kiddies together but she shared her true thoughts only with herself until it came time for them to explode.

Now she was telling him. Now he was listening without crumbling. He looked chilled and pinched. He did not interrupt. Sometimes he nodded, as if he knew how she felt, how she hurt, but he let her go on. She shook her head, she shook her hair, it was hard to be clear even if he listened in the best possible way, and this time she had no complaint about how he listened.

"Probably underneath it all I have deeper feelings about you," she said, and then gasped and jerked her shoulders and added rather frantically: "I don't mean that. I don't know why I have to say that. I don't have to be polite. Why did I say that?"

"Maybe you really—"

"Shush! Listen to what I have to say, not my apologies. After all this time, why can't I just be honest and exact?"

He said nothing. That was better. She smiled a little. She shrugged. She smiled at him across the table because this time he neither argued nor crumbled. She had a favorable impression of her husband just now.

When she smiled at him, he knew what her smile meant. He was allowed to answer. "You think it's all about sex," she said.

"No I don't. You've just mentioned some of the other things it's about."

"Did I? Did you know about them?"

"From the other side of the iceberg," he said.

"Well it's not," she said, "all about sex."

It was late. The child was asleep. It was not so late, but he had stayed for no good reason, for every good reason, because his wife let him put the child to bed and then listen to the truth.

"I'd have liked to be promiscuous," she was saying. "I don't feel free. Is it pride? Is it fear? I think it would be nice, though. Are you promiscuous?"

"That doesn't occur to me," he said.

"I don't like to say I don't care what you do. Personally I would like to think it's all about sex. I don't think so."

"My pride is hurt," he said. "Sometimes I think about sex."

"Don't be angry now. I'd like to live a different way. If I had a clear picture of the future I would try to live it."

"I'm not part of that future."

She shrugged. "I'm trying to be clear. No one's a part of it but me. Sometimes I don't think our child is a part of it. But then I remember she's a part of me."

"I'm not."

"No," she said, "you're not anymore. Or I think you will be again. Sometime far away and long in the future. It makes me so sad when you look so sad. You look so cold sometimes. I wish I could help you."

He touched her fingernail. He pushed at the cuticle. He said: "I'm trying to help myself."

"Me too," she said. "Don't do that to my nail."

He thought: Look how needy I am, like a child. Look how impatient she was, like a child. Look how we have a child we leave out of this. Look how foolish we both are. We loved each other.

"I remember when we used to stay up all night, mussing the bed, and talking, too, till the light came in the windows. I loved those mornings."

"You used to complain how tired you were at school the next day."

"That wasn't complaining. That was bragging."

Now she was pulling his fingernail, massaging his hand. He let his hand rest in hers.

"Sometimes I want to call you at night," she said.

"Why don't you?"

"Because if I do, then you will, too. And you'll think you have the right to call me at night. And I'll wait for your call sometimes. And you'll wait for my call. And then we'll go out to movies. And we'll be dating. And then—"

"Our divorce would be in trouble," he said.

"And then I'll be stuck again. I don't want that. So I wish you could be here and not be here," she said. "Are you here and not here?"

He wondered if she could see through him to the other side. It eased him to know she was sad, too. Was that cruelty? Did he need her misery? No, only to have the feelings he thought she had. He didn't want to be completely mistaken. He was a fool, but he didn't want to feel like a total fool. At least she was not so clear as she seemed.

"I don't like it when you cry," she said, "or look as if you were crying behind my back. But I don't like it when you look as if you were with another woman, either. But I don't care. I just don't like to see it."

"I can't manage to do what's right," he said.

"I like it when I think you're happy with another woman or two," she said. "I'd actually like that for both of us. I don't mind imagining it. I don't like to see it."

This was beginning to contradict what she had been telling him. And she knew it. Nevertheless she allowed herself to contradict what she knew.

They were holding hands like shy swains. They were smiling at each other. "Let us stipulate we are both scared and shy, we both have our reasons," he said.

"Tell me about your ladies," she said.

"Don't be stupid." She pulled her hand away. He retrieved it. "Would you like to be friendly and cuddle?" he asked.

"I'm scared," she said. "I feel friendly, but I don't feel like cuddling with a stranger."

"I know. Me too."

They lay on the floor, and suddenly her slimness was all over him, her tongue darting into his mouth. "What are you looking for?" he asked. "You're fishing."

She laughed. He lay enthralled, an amphibian resting in a pool. "Gently, gently," he said.

She sighed. She nestled her head on his shoulder. "I'm shy," she said. "Let's just cuddle."

"That's what we're doing."

"Thank you," she said.

"We don't have to do anything, prove anything, you see, because I like you."

"I like you too," she said. "So we can do this at least."

Her face and hands were hot and dry. She was feverish, it

seemed. The sweat did not break out on her body. They were both scared. It felt like children not making love. They did not make love. His wife was not his wife; his love was not his love. House, child, memory, marriage, past, present, future, they did not make love. He did not know what this meant. Just then, he felt fine.

"I don't want to make love with you," she said.

"Why did you have to say that? I know. What makes you think I want to?"

"You've been looking at me so strangely these days. I suppose you've got a friend, but you don't look happy."

"You've been looking good. It seems settled. You've got somebody. I've no right to criticize what makes you happy."

"I have somebody to do things with, yes, but—"

She pulled at his hand again in that drawing, massaging gesture, "Just breathe. Just talk. Just like lying here enough."

"I can't promise that's all I'll do."

"I'm having my period."

"That never mattered."

"I feel shy. I don't feel . . . Cuddle," she said, "be careful."

"I used to know when you were having your period. I didn't today."

"How did you know? Was I snappish?"

"Not too much. Just the way you wake up and know what time it is . . . Besides," he said, laughing, "you used to tell me."

"I'm glad you're staying," she said. "Do you mind if I just go to sleep? Just let me hold your hand, okay?"

It was her practical nature. She liked to be kind. She was studying to be kind to herself, too. She needed to wake up fresh for their child. She had a whole life to support with sleep. "I saw an old couple on the street today," she said, "he was old and she was crippled, and they were helping each other across, and it made me feel so sad, so sad, because they're so lucky and we're not . . ."

She lifted his hand to kiss it. He leaned over and kissed her forehead. She seemed to doze. He lay there without moving until he was cramped. She slept. He stood up and straightened his clothes and went to the door. He looked back at her in the dark where she slept. Her breathing was slow and steady. He went to the room where their child slept. He kissed her, and tasted the warm humid sweet breath. He came back and stared at his wife from the doorway. She had turned on her side, curled up. Her eyes were squeezed shut in a dream.

Outside, he looked up at their window. His wife was standing there in a nightgown, waving to him. She was waving good-by. He knew the difference. The wave said she had nothing more to say or do. She couldn't bear his grief. She couldn't bear her own. She wanted to sleep so she wouldn't have to speak. She slept so she wouldn't have to make love. That was not her intention. She just needed to live through this time till she was ready for the new times. That's all there was.

Perhaps, he thought, this is too much burden of communication for a sleepy wave of a hand from an upstairs window.

But oddly enough, it seemed to him as he drove away in the late hour, what she did was right. She was able to sleep. He felt better. He too might rest.

3

THE NEWS said the President had finished his months of Explanation and still nobody believed him, so he was going to take his leave of the country. This struck him as odd. He too was explaining, and he didn't believe himself, and felt selfish and stupid. And his stupidity was more real than the country's pain and the President's nastiness. And this was an incorrect procedure, but he was stuck with it.

Surely, though, he was luckier than the President on the day when his divorce was final. He didn't have to appear. No flight by helicopter and ceremony of spite on the front lawn. The papers were signed by the lawyer they shared, who said, Okay, you're a free man now. My duty is not to speak words of wisdom, since I have none. Go and do things that don't require my services.

She telephoned in the late afternoon, as he sat straightening the staples on a report on I.Q. testing—the existence of alternative forms of English had not been taken into account by Alfred Binet and Theodore Simon and the psychologists at Stanford—and she was asking, "Are you busy?" and he answered Not very, and she was saying, "I'm distressed, dear," and he asked what that meant, and she said, "I keep bumping into things."

"What?"

"Dear, I can't see the furniture because my eyes are swollen. Our child thinks I've got a cold. I'm staying in my room. I'm throwing things away. That's all I can do—*don't!*—" She hung up. She meant don't come to profit from my distress.

Distress. He knew enough now not to forage. He knew he'd be no good to his child, either. He wondered why she had to throw away snapshots and letters on this day. People have a right to be different, he thought, she has a right to be different.

What Jehane had said: *Go and do likewise.* Those were not her words, but it was how he remembered her good advice. "Hang out," she said. "Ride with the flow. Dig the scene. I do not necessarily recommend the singles bars for men with your complexion—liver tendencies is my diagnosis of your polarity, just speaking off the top of the deck. I recommend the singles coffeehouse if you don't use too much coffee. Watch out for that sugar. Anima on the brink. Use milk, not too much cream. And don't wear those baggy pants unless you got an infection, So-called."

"Nervous," he said.

"Nervousness," she said. And she chuckled. "You rascal."

He thought it a sensible idea to spend some time not worrying, not longing, not hoping, not fearing, just hanging out.

"Go and do likewise," she said.

Stupefied as he was by greed for what he had lost, he was

166

nevertheless almost able to figure out what she meant. Ah, that was what she meant.

Model? Artist? Designer?

It was a coffeehouse speculation. He sat with both his hands wrapped for warmth about his mug, comfortable in the knowledge that he could stare at the young woman in the little Danish and Italian espresso monument and she would not see him; she was imperious; no, she was imperial with her slim light body floating someplace inside the beige pants suit, her morning newspaper propped against her own double cappucino, the pink part in her hair shining up at him as he watched from the little shelflike balcony.

Perhaps she was not tall enough to be a model, but she had the slimness, the gawky grace, the light bones and tight skin, the contrasty black eyes and black hair and pale envelope of flesh. She might be a student, she was a serious-student sort—perhaps a few years older, a graduate student—utterly contained within herself as she sat every early morning at almost the same time, reading her paper, silent, always alone. There were no openings. She suggested no openings. There were no hints of an opening or a shyness or a teasing or a fear. She was just doing precisely what she was doing and wanted to do. She sat with the paper neatly folded and leaning against her cup. She ate a bran muffin with butter. Sometimes she ate a croissant with butter. She had a glass of fresh-squeezed orange juice. He drank his own sometimes while watching her from above, so they were both tasting the little floating shreds of orange at the same time—a kind of toast to her in which she did not participate.

Sometimes she left the butter at her plate. Sometimes she took orange marmalade. He discovered no pattern in these choices, but he felt her precision about them.

It was very early. They both needed to be early risers. She enjoyed her twenty minutes, her half an hour of silence, her newspaper folded, and then if he looked away—glanced at his own paper, say—she might be gliding silently out, or she might be gone already, her neat plate, its crumbs, the orange-juice glass left behind like a clue to be deciphered. Her breakfast routine was regular, like his, and her eyelids barely twitched as he stepped gingerly by her for a refill of his coffee. At this hour the place was nearly empty of breakfasters. Together, they shared the silence. For once he had the good sense to leave her alone, perhaps only to nod if a reflex of sound or motion made her glance flick in his direction. For once he had the brains to respect her privacy, and this *for once* lasted for weeks, for months.

The seasons changed and she came to the Morning Kettle alone. Her invisible self-sheltering was something she evidently required. It had a long history, he believed. For once he was somewhat intelligent about a lovely young woman. However he pried in his mind, he stayed away, he did not intrude, he let her follow her own needs.

Twice during this time she violated the rules. They were not rules which he knew she had made; they were rules he had made for her, from watching her over the fall and winter, regular at breakfast, never elsewhere or at another time, drinking her coffee and juice, taking small bites of her small treats, wearing mostly suits which did not hide the slim length of her body, the face impassive, the eyes solemn and complete over the newspaper.

But she violated her habits. One Monday morning she came in with a lover. There was no doubt about it. He was a big russet man with a mustache, urban cowboy clothes, somewhat stained teeth like a devoted urban cowboy. (A teacher in an inner city school? He looked like a practitioner of ghetto do-goodism who told the kids he kept a motorcycle for weekends and expected them to love him for it. Flights of jealous fancy over his coffee near the potted plant on the shelf above them. He was also wearing boots.) The man adored her; that was obvious. He gloomed over her as they took their breakfast. She was smiling, a little paler than usual, not looking at him, and studying her breakfast things as she neatly went through them; he was looking at her all the time. He said something now and then and stared and she answered very softly, with downcast eyes. When they left, the man, who was very tall, put his lanky blue-jeaned arm around her slim shoulders and she submitted to this as they pushed past the later breakfasters. She did not snuggle. She did not protest. She was wearing a filmy suit of some floppy yellow limp material and carrying a briefcase.

She never appeared with this lover again. It must have been the impulse of a Sunday evening, a mistake which she would not repeat. He felt her discomfort with the lover. His jealousy was trivial. He would just like to know how it happened—some acquaintance who had taken her to a movie or to dinner, some loneliness, some insistence, some kindness or generosity for the urban cowboy's need. He felt her regret. She liked to be alone mornings. She was sufficient for herself.

Another time she was there with a woman friend, a somewhat older woman—or did she just look like a graduate student, a model, a designer, a young artist?—with a child. The little girl, aged four or five, could not sit still, of course, but roamed restlessly about the table, and she smiled and teased with her, gave her things to eat, laughed—for the first time he heard her high musical chiming laugh—and her face had shifted into animation, smiling, laughing, listening, concern, while the child's mother told some evidently engrossing story. At one moment she took the child on her lap and hugged her, nuzzling the active little neck. So she obviously knew this mother and child rather well. He noted at the cash register that she paid for all three of them.

But she never appeared with these friends again, either.

On both occasions, adored by a lover to whom she was indifferent, or attending to a friend with a child, she seemed to be in control even of the interruptions in her routine. It was something about the grace and neatness of her costuming; it was something about the way her friends looked at *her*, explained to *her*. And the rest of the time her routine was perfect. Silently she came and went with her coffee, her juice, her muffin or croissant, her newspaper. He loved watching her. He was not content with only this, but he loved watching her, too.

One day, without planning it, as he walked by for a coffee refill, he caught her eye and instead of nodding one quick nod, their usual gesture to say Here we are, we've been seeing each other again, he spoke. "Hello."

She answered with a smile and a nod, but then a very soft Hullo and a smile. White and small her teeth. He nodded and moved on, his heart pounding at so much unaccustomed conversation. He knew the one thing he had done best this year was not to speak with her. It was the wise thing, the prudent thing, the right thing.

But it was also okay to speak that one banal word. I am still being very wise for me, he thought. He returned to his table with his coffee, bent to his own paper, and when he looked up again she was gone. The orange juice glass, the coffee cup, the buttery crumbs of croissant, the unused ashtray. Today she had left her paper behind. She must have stayed longer or finished more quickly. Usually she tucked it under her arm when she left, fitted it between her slim body and the portfolio she carried.

He wondered if she ever saw the urban cowboy, if he was grieving for her.

He wondered when she visited her friend with the lively child who so delighted her.

He was not jealous, of course.

He spied until she went to work, disappeared from his sight, and he also went to his job.

Hello. It was not much of an advance toward a love affair. But it felt like an opening of trust in the coincidence of bigcity life that had thrown them together for breakfast over the months. He was almost content with this one-sided romance. He was luckier than the urban cowboy; he had not yet lost her. Hello, mysterious breakfast companion.

One morning, during the season of the late winter rains, there was a storm and he expected not to see her. Both of them should be sensible, do breakfast at home, pour out the cereal, pour on the milk, brew the coffee, eat the orange or banana, it's not so complicated—why should they be creatures of habit?

But he thought he saw a lull in the storm, a patch of pale blue in the furious blue and gray of the sky, the pelting rain, and he found an old black umbrella in his closet—his former wife and he used to walk under that umbrella—and he leaned his way through the wind to the Morning Kettle. She was installed already, her long straight black hair shining, her high boots purplish with wet, her face cool and her eyes focussed on the newspaper neatly folded and neatly leaning against her coffee cup. This time the empty ashtray had a slip of paper crumpled in it. He got his things, as usual, but didn't climb the few steps to the shelf where he usually sat. He sat at a table nearby. Today they were the only customers. Breakfast was not a busy hour in the Morning Kettle; lunch was busier. The speakers played a morning program of baroque dances, announced by the familiar caramel voice of the announcer who had been doing this since his divorce. He had lost a wife to talk to; he had found FM music in the Morning Kettle.

She was gone.

He stood up and saw her in the rain at the door, struggling with her umbrella. Without thinking, he abandoned his coffee and ran with his own umbrella and his jacket, trailing it by one sleeve as he put it on, and found her laughing and pulling at a blown-out umbrella which flapped and snapped in the gusts. She was laughing at the impossibility of getting the thing to work. "No shelter from this storm," she said.

"Here"—and his big black doorman's umbrella, oldman's umbrella, clicked open and held—"here, get under. We've gotten to know each other, haven't we? I'll walk you wherever you're going."

"It's so wet, what a foolish—"

"I'm out, I might as well get rained on," he said.

He held the umbrella in such a way that she had to hold it too. Their hands were near each other, like kids choosing up sides on a baseball bat. She was still laughing and murmuring, Wet, wet, wet, her wet lips hardly speaking the words.

Under their shelter, black silk tugged but sustained in the rain and freaky gusting, he began to speak. He said, "Tell you something funny, okay? I remember you with a lover—only once. It was a Monday. You looked bored or stuck and you were in a hurry to get away. Another time you were with a friend and a child. You looked the opposite—happy! You were very sweet with that kid. I have a kid lives with her mother across town. I liked the way you were with that child. We have a long history, don't we? So are you a, well, I was trying to think, are you a designer sort of?"

Ducking, she turned to look at him, close under the patterned roof of silk. "Mister Private Investigator," she said, "I work at the Courthouse. I'm the City's hired gun—an assistant D.A."

"You see, I didn't really figure you out."

"But I didn't figure you for such a strong umbrella, either." She had been holding the shreds of hers. She flipped them into a trashcan with bags, cans, and one other skeletal wreck of an umbrella. "So we've been equally ignorant," she said.

"You think it'll last in this wind?"

"That's a powerful machine you got there, Mister."

They were walking, leaning into the weather, fighting the wind and rain, bumping together. She touched his hand on the umbrella. It was no longer like choosing up sides. It was not an adversary situation for the slim assistant D.A. The drops running down her face looked like tears, but they were rain and she was laughing. They passed his automobile parked near his flat. She lived a few blocks further on. They kept on walking.

She was smiling up at him from those dark eyes, that creamy oval self-certain face, and he believed that his long patience might make a difference this time. But she was saying, "I know someone else who wears boots like these ones of yours."

"The urban cowboy," he answered. She looked puzzled, so he went on quickly, "I have a kid, you probably don't know this, comes to visit me on most weekends—"

"You're just exploring, aren't you?" she asked. "Just learning to walk out in the world?"

"What do you mean?"

"You're an innocent," she said. "You're one of those middle-aged boys. You're an old kid."

"I guess that's a way of putting me."

"I like you," she said. "You've been waiting for months to make your move, haven't you? And now we're going for a walk in the rain. Isn't that nice? I like the rain. I like you. But all I want to do, Mister, is have this little walk in the rain. I'm very clear about that. I hope you are, too."

"I am," he said.

"You are *now.*" And she took his arm. Another pal. Jehane was a pal who did the nice dirty things with him. This was a pal who didn't. He needed more.

4

THEN MIRACULOUSLY he heard a voice saying Dearest in the dark night; the voice woke him. It was his own. He was not making love. He was not being loved. He was alone and dreaming. It was not an erotic dream; he remembered no urgent approach. Yes, wet, hand reaching, sticky sheet, it was wet, there must have been some echo of pleasure in the vacancy of his body. Where were the voices? Where was the touching? In his sleep he had been making love with her. He reached. He touched. "Dearest."

Is this madness? he asked himself. Not even that much.

This is self-pity. This is only myself with me.

Other people have sufferings they don't deserve and I can't help. I have no right to these tears.

He was fully awake now.

You have no right to comfort yourself with reasonings, he told himself. Just let the loss soak through and through till you stink of it and can't stand your own smell. And then just shed it in the bath. And get rid of yourself and it.

He thought: I'll not fall asleep again in this mood. I'm not a child—maybe it would be okay for Lester—to fall asleep crying.

After awhile, noticing he was hungry, he went to the kitchen, put on the light, looked in the refrigerator for cheese, Monterey Jack, lettuce, good, a slice of tomato, good, a package of rye bread—good, good—and made a sandwich as if he had wakened from making love instead of only dreaming of it.

The next day, driving to see his daughter, he practiced what he called Broad Scheme of Things Theory: I don't matter that much. When I die, I'll join everybody. While I live, my troubles should be everyone's but are only mine (no starvation, war, crippling disease, sick child, no burden other than a wife who merely ceased to love me). Why don't I turn this massive and generous self-pity outward? There's enough to make me a saint.

He didn't smile at the joke.

What is a rhetorical question? he asked himself. Is it something precise, such as *What is Life? Why me?* or something vague, such as *Do you make your own yogurt?*

He needed a friend with whom he could sort out jokes and questions, receive a smile along with coffee and toast, a laugh and a cuddle.

Yesterday in the teachers' john, he said aloud, practicing, *I read a new graffito: Have You Remembered to Smash the State?*

He thought of the Norwegian wife. He thought of the girl in the coffeehouse. He thought of the tall pretty girl with the straight blonde hair and the band around her forehead, like a Sixties hippie, whom he had seen in the Principal's office. She was a substitute. She wore a wedding band. She smiled at him.

She was married, but the sight of this person made it seem that life should be worth living even if it wasn't.

When he settled his deal with his wife someday, he would try to remember that even at the worst time of his life he had noticed this married substitute teacher with whom he exchanged only one word: "Hi." Then he might remember to smash the state. . . .

Just now, he was busy chatting with his wife. "I think I'm picking on you," she said.

"You are."

"Then why don't you stop letting me? Do you like it?"

"No."

"Because you're so stubborn, dear. You could just give up. You could just go away. You could, oh, hear what I've said. For example, I've heard what you said. I believe that you cared."

He sat waiting. There was the child they shared. There was the life they had shared. There was his wife. How could he go away?

"I suppose it's not in your nature," she said, sighing, shrugging.

He hoped to make her smile. "You used to think I was determined."

"I always thought you were stubborn," she said.

So it was she who had made him smile. All the battles were being won these days. But not by him.

"What I'd like from a woman is loyalty," he said. "I need that."

She nodded. "I can give that," she said. "But I don't want to."

"You're honest, I think," he said. "Or maybe you're cruel."

"I haven't decided which it is myself. You invite me to say and do what I say and do."

"I'd like to invite you to do something different."

Her face crumpled. "I've slid down this way. I don't go back. This is the way I slide, dear. Why don't you just take the child and go out now?"

"Because she's in her room, letting us talk. Because we're talking."

"Okay, okay. Then I'll say this: Don't let yourself be so co-erced by your unhappiness that you don't see me. *Me,* dear. Well, it's not so important anymore if you know about me or not—but what about the school?"

"I pay attention. It's a rule. I do the job. I handle what comes up."

"I suppose that's enough. And how about our daughter?"

"I try to pay attention."

She smiled. "Try to do it better, and then your despair will be less, too, or it'll be deeper and you will even be able to pay better attention to me—won't that be nice?"

She had a confident, stylish way of talking when she was up in spirits and sure of herself. That jokey, intelligent, faintly condescending, stylish way, when she had decided to be up in spirits. She could decide such things. Often she stationed herself a step above him for such conversations; it was easy for her to do so; these conversations often took place on the stairway of their house, in a narrow hall, with his former wife a step or two above and smiling down at him.

". . . or else," she was saying, and he had lost what came before, "you'll be taken to the cleaners, my dear, by the short life we all share."

He was confused. "What?" he asked.

"Taken to the cleaners," she repeated. She wanted him to recognize the essential in his problem. She was fair.

Then, still smiling agreeably, tolerantly, she remarked: "You don't seem to realize my heart is broken, too."

He was stunned. He wanted to touch her, but didn't. He said, "I guess I realize sometimes."

"Well, but everyone's is."

She gave and she took away. She opened and she closed. Her soul was a revolving door.

She was laughing. "I don't believe in making much of my misery, if it happens I have misery. And if I don't make much of it, I don't have it anymore. So I guess you're just different, husband, but I can't worry about you—"

"Don't then."

"—more than I do." She shook her head. "Just live with it like I do, okay?"

"Okay," he said. "And here's our little girl, just sneaking down the stairs, aren't you?"

He opened his arms so the child could jump from three steps away, as she liked to do. It was just enough to feel scared. She liked to play with fears. Now they would go see the ducks in the park.

His wife, this child's mother, seemed often energetic, distressed, lonely, and doubtful about life. She was not sure about her maiden voyage toward independence plus true love. She had begun to suspect that these items were, in fact, full of conflict with each other. It might have helped to pronounce the important adjectival modifiers "ex" and "former" before the words "wife" and "husband," but she too seemed to find these difficult to say aloud, sounding to both of their ears like kike, nigger, spick, wop, words nice people don't like to use. When she tried using the words "ex" or "former" about him, she shrugged and blushed; and when it was in his presence, she felt some sort of complicity, as if they had shared a joke at the expense of the helpless. She didn't like this sharing. It was easier to fall into ironic insistence on *wife*, or *husband*.

She did not change her plans. She never changed her plan. If the plan was impulsive, made in a sleepless night or bored morning, it was nevertheless a plan, not to be changed, not in any basic way. Merrily and charmingly she could dance around it with other, newer plans, but the plan is still a plan. Her plan was to be free and to find true love. Does this make trouble? So be it. Trouble for others? Of course. For herself? Well, let's see. She would not credit herself with courage; let others do that if they liked; but she gave herself a full measure of stubbornness.

"Why are you angry?" her husband asked on his return at the child's bedtime.

"I'm not, really."

"What did I do to you?" No answer for this. "Other than love you and marry you." She shrugged. "That's bad enough, of course, but why angry?"

She sought to be honest with him, and when she was not overjoyed, as now, she became severe with him, too. She was properly and fairly bored. "The only thing that makes me angry is you want me to explain everything."

"I want to understand."

"Why not just accept?"

"It helps me to understand. That's how I am."

"I've explained endlessly."

"I still don't seem to understand," he said.

Severity didn't go too deep. It was a door, too. So she smiled with that merry and charming acceptance of the jolly world; that smile which made everyone feel her strength, her ease, her grace. "Neither do I," she said, "and that's just fine."

Her plan should have been painful for him, but not all that hard to follow. It was painful, but it also seemed hard to follow. This puzzled her. She had not anticipated how his feelings might differ from hers, how he was making trouble she did not really enjoy, how in fact he was someone else entirely from the person she had planned to be her ex-husband.

He felt she should wake up from her plan-making. She felt he should recognize the inexorability of the plans. Their child tried to find an explanation and a plan of her own, and came up with: "Poopoopants Daddy."

"Don't call Daddy names," she said.

"Poopoopants Daddy."

He wanted to show how he hurt. He knew this was foolish. He wanted to be taken care of by a strong woman. He knew this was foolish. He knew he was still merely replying to her, not making his own moves, no matter how often he asked his boring questions; poopoopants foolish fellow.

"The funny thing about me," she said, "is you remember how nice and agreeable I was, and how I wanted to do everything to please you?"

"I loved you for it," he said. "I still do. I remember."

"Well, it's true, I did, and I suppose that misled you. I did it because it made me happy. It put me in control. You were so grateful."

"I still am, retorted the emeritus husband meekly," he said.

"Sometimes I liked it when you joked. But now I only do what I want to do. And when I stop wanting to please you, I stop. And the reason I don't go back on my decision is not because I'm strong. I can't help it. It's just the way I am."

"You're modest and tentative and humble, too," he said.

"These days when you joke, my dear, sometimes it's like a little giggle. Sometimes I really don't like your jokes anymore."

He thought: Tell a man he has no sense of humor and you've lost him.

He thought: Three things used to make a man leave home—a smoky chimney, a leaky roof, and a nagging wife. What does it take now?

He said: "We made history, the fun we had, how we liked

each other, and then our child, how happy we were—"

"That was then," she said. "This is now."

Little room for negotiation. He often said their marriage was in trouble. "No, my dear," she answered this time, "*all* your marriages are in trouble." She was looking at him narrowly. "When you look hurt, I feel bad. I do. So the way I take care of that is to turn my head, walk away, hide, and maybe even dislike you a little. I wish other were the case."

"I wish other, too."

She smiled. "That's better. A little dignity, my old lover."

He shrugged, he spread his hands, he grinned, he shifted from foot to foot, he felt distant and faint.

"Wouldn't it be nice if you didn't spend so much devotion on an errand of mercy to yourself?" she asked. "If you moved on? Collected your things and proceeded?"

"I'm a scarecrow," he said. "I frighten the birds."

"No, you're a lighthouse keeper. There's radar now. All kinds of new ways to look out for things. Your devotion is not required, even if you like to study at your very own storms and rocks."

"I'm not really so fascinated by myself as you seem to think," he said.

That's why I need her. I dream of her arms and their fuzz, her legs tight around me, her convulsion, because I run down by myself. I dream of family and child and home wrapped around me. If I were God, I wouldn't need her. Okay. Stipulate I'm not even holy.

"You're okay like you are, you don't need to look for flaws," she said.

"I've got plenty."

"I meant the opposite of that, dear."

"I may have only one—I'm a bad guy."

"No. I mean if I don't like you, that's not a flaw."

"For me it is."

"I mean it might be my flaw, not liking you, but there it is. So learn to ride with it."

He shrugged.

"You'll learn. You've lost a little too much weight is all my present criticism, dear."

At first he thought her talking to him was nice. Then he realized it wasn't so nice.

"I'm becoming a widower," he said. "You're dying to me."

"Good. Hurry up."

"I'm still in mourning—"

"What it's called is self-pity, since here I am."

"Do you see me at all?" he asked.

"Who?" she answered, and laughed at winning a discussion. When she stopped, she said abruptly, "Don't you think you two ought to go out now, while it's still light? You're just standing here, dear. It's almost as if you don't want to go out with your child but you'd rather stand here talking while I have things to do, chores upstairs, many a mile before I rest, dear. Here's your daughter."

Don't love this woman anymore, he thought, don't care about her, don't think about her, don't don't don't especially don't love her, be in love with her, stay in love with her—in fact, move on and away—she doesn't like you or love you, she doesn't care about you, it's not that she's a bad person, she just isn't interested anymore if she ever was (oh, she was, she was, that's what hurts), but don't love her now or in the future and try not to dwell on the past, if possible, even if the past dwells on me, inhabits me like a termite, a nest of them, but forget her. Think of the nice swinging lope of that substitute in the principal's office. You can admire and take pleasure in that. And your own organs are smooth and not dying, just a little tuckered. So take pleasure in them. And let yourself ride. But don't love that woman. Stop doing this to yourself, since there is nothing favorable in it. Freshen up in mind and spirit. Give up this baggage; drop it. Don't love her. Don't love her. Stop loving her. Say good-by to her. Say hello to yourself and then to someone else. Don't love that one. Don't. Spend a year or two in sleep or hustling around or doing foolish things, other things which will turn out not to be foolish because refreshing—drink, eat, stay up late, fuck, spend money, develop other bad habits, only to keep to the rule—*don't love her now or in the future.*

When this intelligent mania raced through his mind, he felt better. But still he could not fool himself that he was not tired and he longed for the comfort he remembered. Someday it might not matter, but just now it mattered, and the longing pain in his chest, his belly, his heart, his balls was perhaps a chemical cure of love, drawing out the suffering through the cure of suffering.

Is this our Modus Operandi? he thought. Misery, boiling, fat steaming, seasick quaking in the belly? This is a gangster love. This is the M.O. of hell itself.

He took the child's hand.

Once more they fed the ducks in the park.

5

"WHAT'S REALLY, *really* now, you can tell me the truth, your interest in that kid?"

"Who?"

"The black boy. I *axe* you, mister—is he for you or for our daughter, because if the latter, we should at least discuss about it—"

She was grinning. She was dressed in Levis and an unironed blue work shirt. Those fitted jeans and designer blouses really do slim. Now she looked huge with her teasing. He listened to her through the amplification of her clothes. When she stood in front of the closet nude, as she used to, whistling to herself, deciding what to wear, he could pick the character she was putting on for the day by the clothes she chose. When she wore her long cotton skirts and filmy Indian blouses—her Miss-Southampton-on-prom-weekend look—she was gentle and needful.

Today she wore her clothes for tough talk. Miss Phoenix (Arizona).

"Your spitter," she said.

"Don't make stupid jokes," he said. "That's a bad habit you picked up from me."

"I like it when you're angry, dear. Your eyes flash fire."

"What've you been reading?"

"No time, no concentration. Taking stock of my . . . Taking stock," she said. "Oh, I do make stupid jokes, don't I? Just like you."

"Go put on your long shirt."

"What?"

He could pursue this line of inquiry and she could slam him down the stairway and out. So instead he asked, "Why don't we just tell the truth?"

She lowered her eyes. He was wrong about the tough Levis. He could see her lashes wet. "If we know what it is," she said. "We're trying."

Best, he thought, is no clothes at all. How can the best solution be a temporary one? In the long run it doesn't make the truth, but in the short run it seems to.

Her hair was damp and pulled to the nape of her neck, under the collar of the blue work shirt, with a copper clip. This was new. He never tired of her calibrations. He couldn't really know what they meant, and so why this continual study, just because he might know a little and not enough?

The very important thing to remember, he thought, perhaps the most important and essential and could save my life or at least help me not to waste it—*I'm not the first man in this spot about a woman.*

It was hard to get a grasp on this difficult idea.

The difficulty is that for every man there might be a woman he'll follow into the volcano if that's where she's going; and most men are lucky enough not to find that woman: and among the others, those who do, most of the women they find don't need to lead them into the volcano—oh, maybe a little peek of hell, but not the volcano. So only once in a while was there this particular woman and this man.

Just lucky I guess, he thought.

He felt the self-pity draining through the bones of his face like a fresh headcold. He had no use for sinus headaches or pitying himself, but sometimes he did both of them.

"I feel abandoned by you," she said.

"You feel abandoned by *me?"*

"I feel abandoned by you!"

"You wanted your freedom. You wanted a lover. You wanted me out."

"I feel abandoned," she said.

He looked at her and her eyes were downcast but hard and it was true. It didn't have to make sense. It was true anyway. She did not expect turbulence and unhappiness. She had expected marriage. She had expected only the unhappinesses of marriage, not of divorce.

She felt abandoned. How could it be so? It was true.

He murmured softly, cautiously, "I was abandoned by you, darling."

"Oh go to hell," she said.

The shark swam across his cheek. But nevertheless she was sad, she was hurt, she was lonely, and she felt deserted and empty. And she didn't feel what he felt. How could she? Did he know more than his own sad, hurt, lonely, deserted, empty? How could he? Was it the conjunction of their bodies, fingers intertwined, mouths gaping open, gasping and giggling—was that what gave them the genius, it had seemed, to feel what the other felt?

"I'll take the kid now," he said.

"Oh what's the use of talking?"

"I just said I'll take the kid now."

"Thank you very much. Don't come back before tomorrow morning. I won't be here."

He turned away. He would wait downstairs for the child. And suddenly he felt her light cool arms around his neck, her hands pressing against his chest, her head on his shoulder while he looked the other way, and she was saying, "I guess you're responsible for what I want and don't want, for what I get and I don't get, for everything bad and nothing good, and maybe you think I don't feel responsible for all the bad hurt I see all over you as you stand here, and you think it isn't fair, don't you?"

He didn't answer.

"I don't blame you, darling. I wouldn't say anything if I were you, either."

He waited. He felt her hands on his chest, her head on his shoulder. And then he looked down and her hands were gone. Her head was gone. She had run upstairs to find their daughter wherever the child hid out of range of scattered fire.

He stood at the door, waiting for their daughter to come down. He felt all right. He felt good. He felt lightened, not in love, not not in love, loving his child, free of some bondages. A world cannot exist half slave and half free. Well, yes it can, if the world is a person.

He was not in love. He was not bored. He was content. He could contemplate falling asleep forever, mouth falling open, and watching his spirit separate from his body. Maybe he had learned something from the women not in his life.

His former wife came downstairs without their daughter.

What was this?

"I asked her to wait in her room," she said.

"Why?"

"Your friend called me."

"What friend?"

"You have several?"

"I suppose so."

"Joanne. Joan. Jeh-heen. She spelled it for me."

"Jehane."

"Yeah. She offered me a free consultation. It's not all on one side, she said. She said she can't fix your anima without fixing mine. She says she likes to have bodywork—I presume she means fucking, darling?—with both parties to the illness, which she calls wellness."

"That idiot!"

"You son of a bitch," she said.

"Okay, okay, okay," he said. "It's really dumb. I'm sorry she called you. Laugh a little, okay?"

"Why do you think I could just kill you?"

"You're insulted. Your privacy is invaded. Well, you're mad at me anyway for some reason."

"For some *reasons*, mister. No, you haven't got it. It's because you're having fun."

"What fun?"

"Don't play games. You're doing what you want. You're a man and you romp. Most of the time you don't have to feed and dress and worry about baby aspirin and goddamn never stop taking care of a kid. Or when you do, you're a cute divorced father, so loving and tender everyone just can't stand not cuddling you. Shit!"

He had no answer to this accurate analysis. It was what she wanted? She chose it? She took her freedom? She had got what she wanted but it wasn't what she wanted? Once again the aching nerve ripped like a shark through his cheek. She activated the destruction under his eye. He tried to stay level, though Jehane said he should express it all. But his wife expressed it all and it didn't save her.

"Maybe I should just take her now. I'll keep her for the weekend and you can do whatever you want—"

"Great, great. That's a temporary improvement."

His cheek was ripping away. "Well, when I'm at school working all day, and she's in daycare or baby-sitter's hands, you can do what you want—you can find out what you want—you can study or have fun or even *work*, my dear, for some extra money in a two-apartment household, or find true love if such be your mission—"

"Shut up!"

"Gladly."

She stood there trembling. She said: "I'm sorry. I guess I started this. That damn telephone call from a female therapist who enjoyed half the problem . . ."

He tried smiling. "I was ridiculous, too. Isn't it a little funny? You used to laugh at the desperate ones who talked about human potential. I can't tell you how funny Jehane was—also lumpy—not so pretty as you—not my type—really not a big deal."

"Perhaps you've said enough."

He nodded.

"Well, I'll go get her now. If she's heard any of this, she's cowering in her room."

"I hope she didn't. We were whispering. It probably felt like shouting, but we're both pretty careful," he said.

"Great. We're so polite. You have energy for it, don't you?" The motor was revving up again. It was self-cranking, it seemed. All he could do was ride. She had more on her mind and she wanted it out before the weekend began. Maybe she needed to clear some decks. It wasn't just Jehane's call. It was Jehane and more. It was the fate of Woman on her mind. She said: "You have your work. You can get out. You have a whole life away from kid goddamn constant kid."

"I'll stipulate that's true."

Her eyes turned cunning and narrow. "You got me pregnant," she said.

He would not say he stipulated to that. He would not ask her to remember how it was. He said, "It was a collaboration." And despite his resolution, he added, "You seem to forget something."

He could feel the heat now, and the sudden flood of pink, of red to the eye, and that freckling eruption of her cheeks, like when she made love and the capillaries were blinded and burst. "You got me pregnant! You got me pregnant! You got me pregnant!" she screamed.

He wanted to be elsewhere. He was lost with this stranger.

"Don't smile! That stupid smile! You can't run away now! You got me pregnant!" she shrieked, and she was stomping back and forth from wall to wall in the narrow hallway, looking for something to hurt him with. But she had found it long ago.

"Look at me," he said. "What right have you to say this? You're not crazy. You don't have the right to say such things."

"I'm crazy! You're making me crazy! You made me crazy! I was having fun! I was a girl having fun! I wasn't even a woman! You did it!"

"I've been kidding myself," he said.

"That's what you think about, that blessed yourself, while you're killing me—"

"I can stop," he said, not sure he had spoken aloud. "I don't have to go round and round. I don't have to do this. I can give this up. I can stop this murder. I can stop this breaking. I can stop this game. I can end this marriage or divorce—"

"Stop screaming!" she shouted. "Do you even know we have a child?"

Their daughter was standing at the head of the stairs with her mouth open with what must have been tears, must have been confusion and pleading, but he couldn't hear her.

His wife had hold of his right hand in both of her hands, clinging to it, but she was pressing her nails into it, scratching and clawing and twisting as if to break it off, shred it, finish this hand and this person forever. "You did it." She was uttering a hoarse, abandoned, exhausted whisper while, with a very serious and intense grief on her face, she labored at an act of demolition on his fingers and palm and the protruding veins. "You did it," she repeated. "You did it."

It was thrilling for him to discover reflex. He jerked his bleeding hand away from that mashing mechanical work, and she fell against the railing and then to the stairway as the child ran down, screaming, "Don't, Daddy!" and he said to his wife, "Okay now, I've done it," and he had, at last he understood what she was telling him and more, he understood and had made a decision, he had listened to the world and heard the message it was sending, and all that was left was what he was doing now, putting his arms around his child because he loved her and didn't want her to see the blood dripping from the raw gash and punctures and he couldn't see his wife as he put his head against the child's neck and he thought he had better open his eyes, he had better look at his wife, but she had already disappeared, up the stairway.

Part/IV

1

THEIR MARRIAGE was tender, practical, playful, and finally its body was obscured to both of them by the birth of their child and the convulsions of the time. People need freedom, at least I do, she said. Neither of them had expected this. Their divorce was amicable and mysterious.

She had a vision of herself as a Single Parent, fulfilling her destiny perhaps tragically, in the company of other women harassed by history and fate. (But now one could choose.) He had a vision of himself as abandoned by the woman who was once his delight. Suffering little hemorrhages, the day would suddenly be bloodied by loneliness for his wife, for his child.

He kept his daughter with him on Sunday, a claustrophobic, sticky, steamy long day. His daughter took a rest, consented to rest, on his bed. He thought he might nap alongside her. Her rest was only slightly less active than the President addressing both houses of Congress. Frequently she required applause and he came to attention to give it. When she stopped suddenly and smiled into his eyes and touched his face, he longed for her as if she were absent although she was as close to him as a child could be. He missed her just as much Monday morning when she went to school. He visited her on Tuesday and Thursday at dinner-time.

Since this divorce was amicable, which doesn't mean friendly, he took his daughter out of her mother's apartment; or if the weather was bad, the child tired, homework to do, she permitted that they huddle together in the child's bedroom. He told stories. Father and daughter giggled. They used pens, paper, books, records. He liked this game of house with his daughter better than their wandering Sabbaths.

Sometimes his wife—still that trouble saying ex or former— was irritated by the noises they made and would ask him please, please, why don't you just go out someplace? Ordinarily she liked to "de-emphasize" sweets, but in her desperation she even recommended going out for an ice-cream cone. This, he supposed, meant that Single Parent was preoccupied with the obstinacies of a lover or a nonlover. The reactionary character of both nature and civilization was something she had trouble surmounting. She became fretful at such times, sometimes waiting at the telephone, sometimes not liking the telephone when it rang. Men were a burden to her now, and she alternated between jeans and boots and defiant, old-fashioned feminine drag, even to doing her nails and wearing a long skirt. This English country loveliness gave him a pang when she greeted him in it, hair brushed, skin glowing, long arms and legs moving with a grace subtly responsive to the consciousness of good clothes.

He did not understand her. He could not trace the meaning of jeans (rump awkwardly bound by studded pockets), boots, hair awry, against her occasional extravagance of decor. Her behind wobbled when she hustled up the stairs; then the next week she glided ahead of him, elegant and proud. She moved too fast. It was not his business to understand her anymore, especially since he had done such a poor job of it when it was his business.

He was homesick for something he never had. He believed his eyes had gone dead with longing—hers were bright with it. When he looked in the mirror, he found his eyes glistening with fever. He wrote letters to her which she never answered and, though he no longer sent the letters, he still awaited her reply.

Who is older, he wondered, the one with the dead knowing eyes or the one with bright undefeated ones? But then he looked again in the mirror and saw narrow suspicion and anger. *None of the above,* he thought.

Homesick longing for what I can't recall makes a low, mean hope. *I need* is not a complete sentence for a man; it's barely enough to make me forgive Lester his spitting. I want, I lack, I need. But for her too, even for this clever and determined young woman, herself was sometimes a burden.

Happiness and confidence exist someplace in the world. When he thought of them, he thought of laughing with his daughter and Lester. When he recalled the good times with his wife—the meals, the night walks, the lovemaking, the swelling pride and love when she held their newborn daughter and he held them both—he felt only homesick grief. That's no fun, he thought, not worth recollecting. And it did no good to remind himself that his own hunger floated in the great heartsick starvation everywhere else in the world, too.

There was a woman up the street who had lost her daughter to rapid childhood leukemia. It was known on the block; the child had turned pale, turned thin, with huge eyes, and then disappeared; but in the city, people disappear without great reverberation.

One day he came to visit Cynthia and saw his wife walking up the street with the woman who had lost her child. He saw them turn and walk back. He parked his automobile. He watched. They paced off the length of the block and then turned back again. She did not see him; she was listening, listening, intent only on the mother of the dead child. Her face was stern as she listened to the woman tell her story, tell whatever she needed to tell a stranger and neighbor.

It was a shock to him. Her tenderness, her patience, her concentration. He had needed to define her as hard and without care for others, and here she was, not letting herself cry because the woman wanted a careful listener. She was listening.

After a while he went in to their daughter. He could not tell his wife what he had seen and how sad it made him.

In the middle of the night the stupid round-and-round: If I had done this and she had done that, then *she* would have and *I* would have and we might have . . . Such silly conditional and subjunctive occupations for nights of iffing insomnia. It was not much different from nightmare. He seemed to sleep in these obsessions, and once he woke with a wet-winged fly buzzing and bumping against his lamp. He reached up to turn off the light. Maybe he hadn't thought of his wife and only manufactured a dream to go with the fly's irritable bumbling.

He felt that swift deep disgruntlement that overtakes a man whose wife doesn't like him very much. Especially when she once seemed to like him a lot and he depended for liking himself on her liking him; that disgruntles swiftly and deeply. But again he slept and dreamt.

He woke up and reminded himself that the world is lovely, air is to breathe, food and wine to eat and drink, the children are challenging and the teachers a little less so; his body had replenished itself painlessly while he slept; and then, the answer to this argument, something told him that his body was not replenishing itself these nights while he slept, it was turning on bad dreams like bad television, visions of horror like bad movies, an anxious swarming like fearful daydreams. His body was not being good to itself and to him. He needed a swift change.

He tried to whisper his true grief and loss, love grief and love loss, but could not. Instead, he complained and bawled like a snotnosed child. Perhaps he had thought to water her shriveled feeling for him with tears. Wrong. Why should she look up to notice he was present with a nonproductive sinus condition? (Oh, *there* you are! How about some Kleenex?)

The smell of grief pierced far back in his nose, like sour mint, and he no longer knew the difference between this piercing and the smells after love with her, which also had pierced his heart, far back.

He still felt grief and loss. This lover's secret they could not share. No, I'm not here anymore.

He fell silent.

She fell silent.

He lived in slavery. He slipped and struggled, failed to sleep and failed to wake, passed white nights and gray days. This misery came of love, and he hated it. To kill himself—how to do such a thing? with a child he cherished?—was impossible. He wished for an accident so he could not blame himself. Ah, this was foolish. And so he struggled with himself; it replaced the struggle with his wife. He fought against love, he fought against grief, he even fought against anger. They were all linked. He reminded himself when touched, moved, overwhelmed by the sight and smell of her, or a sight and smell which recalled her, or passing their old house or eating their foods or walking on their streets: don't do this, don't feel. First he succeeded in

199

removing her from the struggle; he translated it within, to himself, between himself; then he began to succeed in winning it. He lost love. He lost anger. She became a limited idea, like a newspaper death notice. He did not lose sorrow entirely, but he chipped away at it: don't, don't, don't, he would remind himself in the middle of the night; don't feel; and then dreamlessly he could sleep. Perhaps he dreamt, but he did not remember the dreams.

When he was with another woman, he was only with that woman. He forgot their names, but he remembered to exist only in what happened then and there. The struggle was still within himself. There was no question of love in the pleasure he often felt, a pleasure like dreamless sleep.

When he was with his daughter, he knew who he was. Even with Lester, he had no doubts, he seemed to know.

When he stood on the stairway with his wife, he was something shrunken and foolish. So the solution was to stand there waiting without her. Come down, darling, your dad's here. And alone he was less but better.

He could earn victories by practicing the enjoyment of his daughter, by settling with Lester, by standing on stairways with other women, he could win victories and settle doubts in these ways. And his child refreshed him when his life tuckered him out or he needed more than sleep to wake him and turn him toward liveliness again. The children could still rouse him, this daughter, and also this black kid who looked at him like a father. He no longer imagined accidents which would make the final decision for him.

Nevertheless: the company of grownup women was still required. The scheme was not complete. His wife might not be his wife anymore, but it seemed all the contents of his cells had been reformed in the years when she was his wife. That woman was the one he had craved. Perhaps the form of his cells required her; more likely they didn't, of course. Only *he* did.

He defended himself against the invasions of love and anger. He paid a price.

It was not neat, and that was okay, too. Probably it shouldn't be neat. That would be too dangerous. And so he allowed himself to feel sorrow at the loss of grief. He named it regret, but it was still sorrow. He took a chance in allowing this, but it was a necessary risk. He could no longer be loving, and he had to pay the price of loss. But he could not entirely give up sorrow in order to survive. That would be too much of a price, even in this cause.

And so, with all these penalties and losses, abandoning the goods of hope and joy, risks of love, risks of anger, thickening memories day by day and year after year, he believed life was now once more worth living. There was the air of early morning. There were certain tastes. He climbed into the newspaper with a certain satisfaction: other lives out there, a nervous large world. He treasured his hours with his daughter. It was interesting, he thought, very interesting indeed, that these things could be enough for a man. In the past he would never have believed it. He had expected something different. This, like the newspaper, constituted very interesting, distracting, objective information.

He read the regret which lay beneath as he read the obituaries in the newspaper. It was not grief, and yet it was still grief. It was merely regret for the disappearing past, rapidly diminishing into itself without his participation.

The chief rule for rescue of himself was not to think about her. That was essential. He began to succeed in this enterprise —not remembering, not imagining, not conjecturing, not taking an imaginary place in her life. He began to succeed. As compensation for this withdrawal from her, he could think more about himself. What might have been a boring vanity seemed to become—an interesting vanity. For example, when he thought about himself, he was surprised at the success with women obtained by a melancholic, bedraggled, preoccupied, recently divorced, gray-flecked man. They liked him! (Some did.) They wanted to help. There is often something agreeable about a disaster. The pretty little substitute teacher with the beaded Indian band around her hair, like a Sixties Pawnee, and what was that? kohl around her eyes? smiled brilliantly, listened, and nodded in time with his complaints. She was so fresh and pretty. She smelled so clean. She said, *I hear you*, when he had the nerve to say he had had a hard time.

He should have come to rest with the Sixties Pawnee who liked him a lot and smiled more and more brilliantly, consolingly. He even liked her. She seemed to know he liked the beaded band, didn't like the kohl; kept the band, erased the kohl; an insightful and sympathetic little slip of a woman. He liked her as much as he could. However, he didn't really care about her and the other women with whom he had this success. And this was probably the reason for his success.

Or maybe these women just liked to gather round the disaster for the fun of it—watching the building crumble and entranced by how the embers will flare up.

Sometimes, when all the conjunctions were right, his wife invited him to sit at the kitchen table, to have dinner with her and their daughter. He had no pride. When she asked him, he did, although afterward he often felt a new sharp sadness within the melancholia he carried almost by habit these days. It would be seasoned for a time by fresh regret. Nevertheless, he had to eat, didn't he? Even at the butcher-block table they had chosen together one Saturday afternoon in May—didn't he? Where on other evenings, and no doubt at breakfast, her lover Hal also leaned on his elbows and let her serve?

You're still seeing him? he asked.

Who? What?

Hal.

Oh, him, she said. Trying something, I guess. Trying not to be lonely, you know?

I was lonely, he said.

She shrugged. So is Hal sometimes. Three lonelies don't necessarily make a right.

He laughed.

But since you ask, she said.

He waited.

Have some more hamburger, she said, it's chopped steak, it's a case of little fat and no extender in this household.

After the evening when he asked, she seemed to feel free to speak of Hal when it occurred to her. She said, He's easygoing; or, He leaves me alone; or, He teaches me new things; or, He doesn't shove and push . . . She never said she loved him. She never said anything about wanting him to be her love.

He teaches me new things?

He would not be jealous of an instrument. It was an instrumentality. It was someone who didn't get in her way. She didn't know what her way was. Hal helped her along her way. It was a guide, a signpost, a symbol, not a person.

And yet, that direct gaze, that cheerful sad cool gaze, was not without puzzlement. She realized love existed someplace. She had loved him once. She had not praised him by saying he was easygoing (he wasn't). She had praised him by saying she loved him.

Good girl, she said. Good former husband. You both finished your dinner. You joined the clean plate club, both of you. I'm proud of my family.

Mommy, *you* didn't! said the child.

I can save it till tomorrow. I can have it for lunch. That's my privilege since I make the meals around here.

After this supper—another Single Parent improvisation of

hamburgers and tomatoes and fruit and warmed-over coffee—
she asked if he would like to put their daughter to bed. He
would. He stayed. He wondered if she merely wanted a burden
lifted, the one of goodnights, glasses of water, important Nursery
School gossip, but no, he smelled fresh coffee, he heard the
grinder, she was making coffee.

She didn't offer him any yet. When he came back from their
daughter's bedroom after the last, final kiss, and the one after
that, and said goodnight, thanks for the dinner, she asked:
Would you like a glass of wine?

Yes.

She wrestled with the bottle. Would you decork it?

Yes.

He sank into the grandfatherly chair which used to be his. She
sat on the couch and crossed her legs and uncrossed them and
smiled. He thought how long it had been since he had seen her
lips and teeth slightly stained by wine, and how nice it used to
be when they sat looking at each other, thinking they understood each other without words, not understanding each other
even with words, smiling, loving each other and drinking wine.

She patted the pillow beside her on the couch. Come here.

Obediently, good dog, he came to sit beside her. He asked a
question about their daughter's school. She shook her head stub-
bornly, that was not it at all, and her eyes were also smiling at
him, as she said: Your lips and teeth are pink.

They kissed very lightly. He tasted the wine on her mouth.
If it was pink on his mouth, it was red on hers.

During the first months of their separation, almost until their
divorce was final, they occasionally made love. At first he
thought this a reconciliation and she would fall into a rage about
his presumption. Then he took it only for what it was, as she said
he had to take it, but he would grieve when he went home to
his own bed afterward, which was where she wanted him to go.

A few times, when he was especially distraught with regret for the lost dream of true love, she watched him with narrow eyes, how boyish of him, and offered him a sympathy fuck. He accepted this several times. Then, although she never reproached him for it, he learned it was better not to accept it.

Now time had passed, he was familiar with sleeping alone, he was familiar with sleeping with many different women, either was okay, he was used to his life. He could say little more than that he was used to the second half of his life.

So when she, on this autumn evening more than two years after their divorce, in a way he dreamily recalled from the time of separation, decided they should now make love, his thoughts were: Not to be depressed tomorrow. Not to make anything of this. Not to care.

With these negatives in mind, too much freight for fun, he felt somewhat dulled and lacking in energy. But it was easy and comfortable to hold her in his arms, to rock her, to stroke and knead her with his hands, with his fingers, while her arch twisted and her slipper fell off, to kiss her not very much but to breathe on her and let his mouth follow the pleasant paths of her body. Suddenly she jumped up. He waited. Ah. Something she surely had to do with other callers: make sure the child was asleep.

Then she went to the bathroom. When she returned, she was wearing only a robe. You're still dressed? she asked. Come.

He said: No, come here.

He didn't want to go to their bed.

She let him play with her. What he did was not so much make love; he was thinking of other things, even of other women, bright beads around the Pawnee's high narrow skull, although with other women he often thought of her; it was not love he was doing with her. He was too dreamy and distant. He was overweighted with negatives. He simply engaged in diddling.

Surely she felt his abstraction.

He thought about the fatigue of driving home after lovemaking, the definition of the bachelor—he comes home from a different direction every morning—and he was in no hurry to leave off the repetitious, gentle, professional gestures he was performing. He could have been a masseur or a doctor. Nevertheless, he remembered her body, and he knew where to go. But he didn't go there. He simply played, in and out, round and about, treading byways, marking out the slim-fleshed skeleton.

He smelled the wine.

He smelled the coffee from the kitchen.

He smelled rich, thick female smells of pleasure saturating her body. He didn't care. He smelled arousal on himself. He didn't care. Where did you learn that? where did you learn that? Oh, it's good, she said.

He didn't care to answer, but he climbed into the rhythm of what he was doing, let the metronome tick, and he did it and did it, now thinking not about others but about her. But not thinking very much about her. She was just there. He was just there. And they were just making love.

And then it happened. She began to scream and toss and heave her body—thinking of other things, he had moved himself to press against the place which always relieved her toward sleep —and her eyes were open, her mouth was open, her tongue was longer than he had known, now her eyes were squeezed shut and the scream seemed to come from an absence. . . . Shush, he said, you don't want to wake—

Oh, oh, oh.

And then she subsided. When she seemed nearly asleep, he guided her to the bed, her head resting on his shoulder, drowsy, like a little girl too long in the bath, and he tucked her in and said goodnight. No, he said, he would not stay. She smiled. He went to the kitchen and took a swallow of the cold coffee from the Pyrex pitcher. He left.

Driving home, he took to his old bad habit: ruminating. Figuring it out. He called it thinking, but it was more like an obsessive daydream, the foolish unquenchable child in the gray-flecked man. She had smiled in relief because he was not staying, because he was not making the mistake of making anything of this. Well, he knew. He might be stupid, but he could be educated.

This time perhaps he really had been thinking.

And so they formed a habit.

Not on every visit ("visitation"), but perhaps once a week, or maybe twice, when it seemed convenient, he would make love to her, he would make a love drill, a love exercise with her, when it seemed convenient, if she had nothing else for the evening, if he had nothing else for the evening. They never discussed it. She seemed deeply grateful at first, not for the lovemaking, of course, which was her due, but for his making nothing more of it than what it was. She was confident in her climaxes—not the little whimpers of their marriage, but howls and thrashings and bitings. She was probably sure he wouldn't do this again and again unless he also wanted to. And of course he did want to, although he was not sure why.

We were both trapped, I see that now, she said.
How?
By love. By playing games.
I don't see how those things go together, he said.
You wouldn't, she said.
He could put up with insults. This was progress. It made him feel much better to listen and not to care, to hear her thought and yet stand where he stood. And anyway, she meant no insults, that was his old way of thinking about it. She was simply thoughtful in her certain way. She was in the business of peeling

scales from eyes, and of course this might hurt sometimes.

Nevertheless, what he answered was: I wasn't aware of playing games with you. I was aware of being in love with you.

You would be, she said.

He smiled and shrugged. Stipulate that, he said.

Used to be, she said.

He smiled and said nothing.

Good, she said.

Her slim, lank body began to feel like beef under his fingers, his tongue, his body. He was far from all this, but nevertheless he understood that something new was happening to him, to this person who was far from what was happening to him. He was glad. He was careful not to show too much pleasure. He had liked to laugh and chatter and roar when they made love. Now he said nothing, he tended to business, and at his own climax, he stifled his moans and only his rasping breath could have been recorded. He did not feel it would be polite to give her words of love; not polite to her, not polite to himself.

It was supremely okay. His melancholia was lifting. He enjoyed his girlfriends, and would laugh, chatter, and roar with them when the occasion arose.

He began to feel well at last. In a way, he had a family. The long Sundays with his daughter were filled with adventures—roller-skating, children's theater, picnics—and he enjoyed them, and enjoyed dropping her back at her mother's house. Once he even took a shower before he made love to his former wife; never, however, would he stay the night afterward.

For that whole autumn she seemed bemused and at rest, and waited with no impatience, not entering into the games, when father and daughter played. When he heard the grinder and smelled fresh coffee, he knew this was one of their evenings. He put the child to bed (goodnight, goodnight, sweet thing). He went in to his wife. He liked the smell of the coffee, but if they didn't drink it first, he usually didn't warm it up later.

He was very patient with his wife. He fell into a state of abstraction. He would notice almost with surprise that he was aroused, and that he was very aroused, and that suddenly this was an extreme of pleasure. Sometimes she scratched and clawed at him. Once she lay there shuddering, pulling the blanket up to her chin, and asked if he would like to spend the night, they could cuddle and just sleep—

I'm not tired, he said. I don't think I could sleep. I would disturb you.

That's all right.

It would be confusing for *her* to wake up in the morning and find us . . .

You're right.

When winter came he began to wonder if this would go on forever. It did not interfere with his affairs with other women; at least, he thought it didn't; but he felt nothing much but laughter or pleasure with the other women. However, that had been the case before, too. And the depression seemed to have lifted. Or at least he thought it had.

Sometimes he wondered what this must be doing to his wife's search. Was she free? Was she free of love and marriage? How was Hal finding her these days? Was she free to be herself alone? Perhaps she was.

And then one night, eyes flashing, she asked, as if it were a great joke: Why don't you ever take me to the movies?

And he repeated an old story: Because I think our marriage is in trouble.

Acknowledging their divorce, they went on making love. He was not sure she meant the joke the same way he did. Of course, since they never had understood each other, this was in their tradition. And now that he had stopped trying, he too took pleasure, relish, even excitement, in making love to this stranger who, he used to think, was the closest person to him on earth.

Now, of course, their daughter was the dearest person, and as to the closest, there was no one.

She got up one night as he sat drinking cold coffee in the dark before the drive home. Your shoelaces are untied, she said. Who usually does them for you?

I usually tie them after the coffee.

She bent and deftly made neat tight bows and then sat up and took his hand. Do you forgive me? she asked.

You're not a sinner. I'm not a judge.

But do you forgive me?

Sin's not a part of it.

Then you do?

No. Never. But I don't think I blame you, either.

He took his hand away from hers. He looked at the child's things stacked neatly in the corner—puzzles, books, games in clumsy boxes.

He said: I blame myself. I'm glad I loved someone, even if it would kill me to lose like this ever again. I don't forgive myself.

So you're not going to take the chance again? she asked.

He shrugged and didn't answer. He looked at her, smiled, and didn't answer.

Well, I forgive you, she said. She too was smiling. I find that easy to do. We find different things difficult, don't we, dear?

On this cold late night, as he drove homeward through deserted streets, between brick walls that were silvery in the weather, and the damp glistening on the streetlights, he found himself uttering a questioning prayer: Not by might nor by power, O Lord, nor by love, does the spirit turn; but by indifference?

It was the only time during those months when the old sadness returned. This prayer brought back all the misery of loss.

For the next two weeks he left as soon as he said goodnight to their daughter.

Why are you so busy these days? Are you in love? she asked him.

No, just busy, he said.

But then they began again. It was like lovers returning together after a vacation. And he did not begin on her on the couch and then go to the bedroom. He led her to the bedroom, or she simply walked to the bedroom, dropping her clothes, and he followed, dropping his own clothes in a careless pile near the bed, near the dresser which used to contain his socks, shirts, underwear and which she now used for all the new things she had bought during her periods of more elaborate decor.

He returned naked to that pile of clothes in the dark, dressing rapidly as she slept, slipping down the stairs and out into the cool nighttime street, and then breathing deeply, his face to the sky, before opening his car door.

Let me pursue where love leads, he thought, so long as it is not love. And this is not a prayer, he thought, it is an observation. He did not want another episode of sullen grief, when he prayed for death, only asking that he not have the responsibility of it. Now he took the responsibility for following out whatever might emerge or be given.

And then he felt the grief again. Because there seemed to be no way he could bury it, drown it, stifle it. Why? Why now? Why this time? Because he had loved his wife with the passion of his life. And now he indifferently stroked and played at her body, and waited for her to claw and shudder against him; and then, out of politeness, and also so that he might sleep afterward, he allowed himself the modest shudder of pleasure.

One night, after they had finished, both finished, finished both of them together (this was rare), she did not sink into that famished sleep of hers. She lay awake, her arm askew so that one hand rested on his shoulder, cupping it, and she asked if he was hungry. No. Sleepy? No. Would you like something to eat? Thank you, no. Would you like to stay the night—and her hand tightened on his shoulder to keep him from answering too fast —and have breakfast with both of us?

I don't think that would be a good idea.

His wife fell silent. They had agreed that to raise the hopes of their child would be frivolous. They were serious parents.

She was breathing shallowly, with a catch at the end of each breath, as she started to say something and stopped. Finally she said it. What is all this about?

Nothing, I suppose.

Why are you doing this?

He almost felt angry. That is, he remembered how anger used to feel, the rising flush and turmoil, but of course he did not allow himself to feel it. Why are *we* doing this? he asked. Because we want to.

Because you want to and I do, too, she said.

Okay, if you like.

Is that all? she asked.

He did not like this conversation. It had the pattern of the repetitious explanations of early separation. I admit I want to, he said. We can stipulate that.

But why is that all? Why has it been so good?

Is it? Because.

Tell me. Talk to me.

There's no one to call to account. That wasn't what I used to like. It means we're free.

It sure does, she said. Is that what you want?

It's perfect. It's rational. You're a sensible woman. It just happens that you want what I want, and together—

I should feel terrific.

Don't you?

I don't know if there's a way to get away clean, she said. I wonder if I'm ready for that.

You're still wondering? he asked. I'm the one who wonders. You're the one who knows.

Hey. Is this all?

Here in the dark, hardly seeing each other's faces, hardly speaking until tonight, trembling and convulsing and sleeping and fleeing, it had been good, as she said.

Why? she asked. Are you a stranger? Are you gone? Are we released? Is that why?

And he answered: "Because I don't like you very much, my darling."

She was smiling as she lay her head on his shoulder. The smile was not ungentle, it was even kindly, the smile of a woman who might someday grow older, they both might grow older, and it would be helpful, wouldn't it? if they came to the end of warfare. What she said was: "Not another sweet word, darling."

And what she then said, still with that gentle, that not ungentle smile: "You'll wreck things, don't you know, if you pretend it's up to you."

DATE			
NOV 27 1980			
JAN 2 2 1981			
SEP 3 '81			
DEC 2 3 1987			
MAR 0 2 1989			